THE WEIRD SHADOW OVER MORECAMBE

Professor Mandrake Smith would be unrecognisable to his former colleagues now: the shambling, drink-addled erstwhile Professor of Anthropology at Oxford is now barely surviving in Morecambe. He has many things to forget, although some don't want to forget him. Plagued by nightmares from his past, both in Oxford and Papua New Guinea, he finds himself drafted by the enigmatic Mr. Thorn, whom he grudgingly assists in trying to stop the downward spiral into darkness and insanity that awaits Morecambe — and the entire world . . .

EDMUND GLASBY

THE WEIRD SHADOW OVER MORECAMBE

Complete and Unabridged

LINFORD
Leicester

First published in Great Britain

First Linford Edition
published 2014

A catalogue record for this book is available
from the British Library.

ISBN 978–1–4448–2229–8

1

Wednesday, December 8th, 2004

For the past eighteen months, the old man had wandered the streets of the increasingly derelict Lancashire coastal resort of Morecambe — contender for the unenviable title of 'The most depressing town in Britain'. None of the Morecambrians knew where he had come from, for none had ever stopped to speak with him, his mysterious background becoming the stuff of local lore. The few who were aware of him speculated that he was a re-housed murderer or a paedophile living out his miserable existence in a nondescript squat somewhere along the West End — the great haven for the dole-dossers, junkies and other down-and-outs.

Those with a less judgemental outlook saw him as but one more unfortunate: a pitiful, wasted man — one of society's forgotten — eking out a shadow of a life, like them, in a gloomy, largely boarded-up town. One rumour had it that he was Scottish, an outcast from Glasgow, though what he had done to achieve that lofty status remained merely whispered conjecture, as this assumption was based solely on the fact that he sometimes wore a tartan scarf and was never seen without a bottle of cheap whisky.

Heading for the promenade, the fingers of his right hand were clenched around one such bottle; whilst the fingers of his other hand, deep within his scruffy coat pocket, gripped the white pharmaceutical bag which contained more than enough painkillers to bring his extraordinary life to an end. He could have decided to nestle down in one of the bus shelters and indulge in his overdose there, but the fear of being noticed and perhaps revived prompted him to make for his squalid abode: a basement room of the now heavily vandalised and dilapidated Midland Hotel — where, in private, he would commit suicide. There was nothing left for him; nothing but the unending nightmares and the dark knowledge which seemingly he alone had to endure.

The sky was darkening as deep grey-black clouds roiled and gusted inland, carried on the strong, biting winds that swept furiously landwards across Morecambe Bay. Spits of light hail began to fall from the cold winter sky.

'*Oi!* 'Pervy' Stan!'

With a painful crack, a hurled egg shattered off his back. Fragments of shell and a splash of yolk flew over his left shoulder. He turned, just in time for a second egg to strike him. Like the first, it too shattered, tiny pieces of shell nicking his cheek.

A gang of adolescent schoolboys, still in their uniforms — their jumpers torn and frayed, their ties out of place — yobbed about before him. Some laughed like hyenas, whilst several others pulled faces and made rude gestures. Their ringleader, who had thrown the eggs — an acne-faced youth of about fifteen — drew his arm back, readying his third missile.

Like a white blur, the egg sped forth and smote off the old man's forehead, drawing blood and an outburst of cruel laughter. Feebly, he tried to shield himself

3

from further attacks, but the eggs were now coming thick and fast as others in the gang leapt in to attack. By the time he had staggered out onto the main street leading towards the promenade, he was dripping in egg, bits of shell in his hair and inside his unwashed shirt.

Still the hooligans taunted him, harrying him and pursuing him. Normally their missiles would have been hurled against shop windows, allowing the brave throwers ample time to make good their escape; but 'Pervy' Stan, as he was unaffectionately known around town, was just too tempting a target.

Bracing themselves against the growing wind and hail, what few bystanders there were looked on with complete indifference. With a curse, a dark-coated man stepped from a shop doorway and bumped into the hapless victim. An elderly couple on the other side of the street, hauling their shopping trolleys, stopped and actually started to clap. This was the poor man's Blackpool after all, and until the Bingo halls opened one had to make the most of free entertainment.

Besides, it was better to be with the mob than against them — no one wanted to intervene and risk attracting their wrath and suffering a similar fate.

Having now run out of eggs, the schoolboys jeered and spat out names. Their fun over for the time being, they quickly forgot their victim and headed for shelter in the *Oasis* amusement arcade.

Ignoring the torrent of public abuse and fighting back the misery, 'Pervy', hurt, angry and humiliated, staggered on, half-blinded by the wind and rain. Blood trickled from his gashed forehead as he was forced off his chosen route and towards another dingy back street. Here the ground was slick with rain and litter. Torn bags filled with domestic rubbish lay strewn all over. The wind was now approaching gale force, raising discarded crisp packets and burger boxes in miniature whirlwinds. Behind him, a bin overturned, its dented lid and a collection of beer cans sent rattling along the cobbles.

Distant thunder rumbled ominously as the sky turned an unwholesome shade of black.

Slipping on the wet ground, he went down, cracking a knee against the hard stone. Painfully, he got to his feet, relieved to feel that the bottle he had shoved into his pocket had not smashed on impact. It, and the pills in his bag, remained his sole passport out of this tortured existence.

The rain was coming hard now, his dismal surroundings veiled in what seemed to be a wall of water. Rainwater gurgled and rushed along gutters. Tiles from one of the unoccupied squats over to his left seemed to launch themselves at him as though hurled by a malevolent poltergeist, smashing into smithereens as they struck the ground and walls nearby. With a terrified hiss, a startled cat darted past.

Exiting onto another main street, he was struck by yet another violent blast of wind, which almost knocked him off his feet. Gusted along, he managed to support himself against a lamp post, the cheap estate agents and the tacky hairdressers he was now passing on his right creating havens of bright light in the growing darkness. Some interested faces glanced out at him, but apart from himself the streets were now empty of pedestrians.

Stepping off the kerb onto the road proper, he was startled by the screech of tyres and the angry blast of a car horn. A window rolled down and an irate, bearded taxi driver hurled more than a few choice words of protest before accelerating off, catching 'Pervy' in a further spray of freezing cold water.

For someone who no longer cared for his own life, he did his best to avoid harm — considering that he could just as easily have waited for the next passing vehicle and then leapt out, head first, in front of it. But, in truth, he was too scared to die in such a manner. He was far too squeamish, his fear of blood preventing him from committing suicide in too 'messy' a fashion.

On numerous dark evenings, after he had awoken screaming from the nightmares, he had just sat on a filthy lavatory, his entire body, and in particular his right hand which held the shining razor blade to his left wrist, trembling uncontrollably.

He had once contemplated leaping off the Stone Jetty at high tide, hoping that the chill would take him before he submerged and drowned, but had finally opted to take an overdose. In his feverish, tormented mind that was the only way to be sure — to guarantee success. Besides, if done properly and with copious amounts of whisky, he reckoned it would be virtually pain-free.

He was now in a large empty car park — a closed down market — behind the neglected Winter Gardens and the Pleasureland Arcade. Exposed to the storm's rising fury, he had to lean into the wind, his grizzled face a portrait of misery and despair. A faded caricature mural of Stan Laurel and Oliver Hardy looked on unsympathetically, their usually jovial faces eerily altered by age and the weather.

The lashing from the rain had wiped most of the egg remnants away, but he was now drenched from head to toe, his bedraggled hair lying in sodden strands. He was entering a covered alley, a walkway between two cheap shopping areas, that was filled with wind-blown litter and stank strongly of urine.

Despite the grim conditions, a flash of garish crimson caught his eye. So bright and out of place, the image struck him with the intensity of a flash bulb. Blinking, he turned to look.

In crudely daubed words, a scrawl of blood-red graffiti on the wall read:

PREPARE
FOR HE IS COMING

The rain drummed incessantly off the corrugated roofing of the covered alley as the channelled wind buffeted down the passage, threatening at any moment to lift him off his feet. Each forward step was laborious, like wading through thick tar. Doggedly, he pushed on into the wind, the welcoming sight of the War Memorial and the run-down, abandoned Midland Hotel barely visible on the other side of the main road which was the Morecambe front.

Built in the early 1930s, the Midland Hotel was one of the first Art-Deco Oliver

Hill-designed buildings in Britain, having replaced the North Western Hotel built some eighty years earlier. It had been an impressive architectural gem of the north, built at a time of great social uncertainty as a positive symbol of grandeur, progression and hope. A predominantly white, curved, three storey structure, its entrance roofed by twin seahorses, it had played a prominent part in the town's tourist trade of the 1930s to the 1960s, having had such notable visitors as Laurence Olivier, Wallis Simpson and Coco Chanel. Even in its waning years David Suchet, in his role as Hercule Poirot, had graced its doors.

That was then, however, and this was now. For now it lay shrouded in large wooden boards, scaffolding, **KEEP OUT!** signs and plastic sheeting — a symbol no longer of hope, but rather of decline, decay, and the ill fortune that had befallen Morecambe. It was an eyesore to those who remembered how it had once been and even those who did not, its opulence and beauty now consigned to a nostalgic period in the past, to a time when Morecambe used to have a fairground which boasted the second-tallest Ferris wheel in Europe, illuminations, a *Tussaud's* wax-works, and two piers. The sole remaining entertainment venue was *The Dome* — a white, inverted bowl-like structure that played host to those stars and celebrities who could not get a gig at Blackpool.

Many regarded The Midland as the 'heart' of Morecambe — the gauge or barometer which measured the town's prosperity and holistic health. If so, the undertakers had not been informed, for the hotel looked like the skeleton of a murdered dream. The town was now a graveyard by the sea and, despite all the optimistic talk from the council about refurbishing, regeneration and redevelopment, people no longer believed it. There would be no phoenix-like rising from the ashes for Morecambe — not whilst all the country's millions kept going 'down South'.

Still, as far as 'Pervy' was concerned, it was home.

And, as soon as he got in through the rotting boards at the rear of the building and into his damp basement squat, where he could climb into his dirty sleeping bag and take his final, lethal drop of 'medicine', it would become like Heaven.

★   ★   ★

Even as the Midland Hotel's most recent guest clambered into his only remaining sanctuary with the intention of taking his own life, less than five miles away on the exposed Middleton Sands an equally unfortunate man by the name of Trevor Whitcomb was running for his life. The storm out here on the tidal barrens was ten times as bad — the darkness, with no street, shop or house lights to be seen, was enveloping and threatening. Distant lightning crackled.

At thirty-nine, Trevor was a relatively fit man, having spent several years in the army before being invalided out after receiving a sniper's bullet in the shoulder during his first tour of Northern Ireland. The strong, salty tang of the sea, mixed with sewage and chemical effluent, assaulted his nostrils and stung his eyes, making them weep.

He could sense that something was close on his heels and that, despite his actions, it was gaining on him. Shingle crunched under his trainers, shifting awkwardly and impeding his flight as he tried to stop himself from tripping. In addition, large, irregular-shaped pieces of driftwood, old tyres and other heaps of assorted flotsam littered this stretch of beach. Rounding a spur of headland, the ground gave way to a stretch of firmer sand, allowing him to increase his speed. Through the rain, he could see the bright lights of the two Heysham nuclear power stations well over a mile distant along the coast. Over to his right, rearing like a dark fortress, were the grim ruins of the old *Pontins* complex. Now abandoned, the chalets, the swimming pool and the amusement buildings had fallen into complete disrepair. It was fit for nothing — even its proposed use as a medium-security young offenders' prison had been rejected. Nonetheless, this was where he was headed, well aware that the predominantly featureless beach offered no cover. He knew that he could not outrun that which was in pursuit. His only hope was that he could hide somewhere within the derelict holiday camp.

Looking up, he could see that a large wall, formed almost entirely from huge breeze blocks, ran along the top of the cliff, preventing access to the forsaken leisure site. Cruel-looking razor wire coiled along the top of the defence. Here and there the wall had crumbled, eroded along with the cliff edge, and in such places the county council had hammered boards over the gaps along with numerous **DANGER!** and **KEEP OUT!** signs. Some of the warning signs depicted images of German Shepherd dogs. Skull-and-crossbones signs saying **ACHTUNG!**, a machine-gun tower and patrolling sentries would not have looked out of place.

Fiercely, the rain struck his back as he started the climb; fallen rocks, portions of collapsed wall and a jagged spider's web of rusty, tangled steel cable-work formed a crude ladder of sorts. He was nearing the top when his feet slid from under him, his knees cracking badly on the slick, sharp cement. Desperately, he grabbed hold of the ragged slab of tumbled wall, saving himself from a painful slide on his chest. Frantic, he began to pull himself up, feet searching for a purchase.

His hands were bleeding, the flesh deeply grazed by the time he reached the base of the wall. All was shrouded in darkness. The sharp throbbing in his left knee, where it had jarred on his ascent, was excruciating now that he was putting weight on it. Gritting his teeth and fighting back the pain, he limped over to the nearest part of wall that was covered by boards and began to desperately tear at it. The wooden patchwork defence came away readily. Throwing a board aside, he ducked down and went in.

Shadowy rows of drab, uniform chalets stretched out before him, their paintwork peeling and defaced, their windows either smashed or boarded up. Glancing quickly to his left, he could see that the chalets extended in that direction for quite some distance before ending at a neglected crazy golf course. To his right, a second row of chalets ran perpendicular to the ones near him, all of them in a terrible state of disrepair. Grass and weeds grew to knee height in the once-pristine lawns between. Old pathways were covered with broken glass.

Knowing nothing of the camp's layout, Trevor decided to just try and get as much distance between himself and the perimeter wall as possible, reckoning that once in the tenebrous, abandoned interior, he would be in a far better position to find somewhere to hide. He hobbled forward, moving as fast as his discomfort would permit.

Several large buildings loomed before him. One was the remains of the old swimming pool, every single one of its windows shattered, its paintwork hanging from its walls like diseased skin. Not far from it stood what had once been a two hundred-seat theatre and ballroom. A large hulk of a building, built on slightly raised ground, it had been designed to resemble a small ocean liner complete with a red funnel and numerous porthole-style windows. In all likelihood it was the nearest thing to an ocean liner that anyone for miles around had ever been on — a grounded ship which, like the locals, was going nowhere; disintegrating and waiting to die, if not already dead. And yet, the so-called *SS Berengaria*, as fading lettering above its main entrance still managed to declare, had once been the focal point of the entire holiday complex. In the camp's heyday, predominantly during the 1960s, the theatre had borne witness to gala performances, televised events, Miss Britain contests, Wurlitzer organ competitions, ballroom dances and numerous other forms of extravaganza.

It was now about to become a mute spectator to something altogether different.

Trevor's heart sank to see that the main doors were secured by a large padlock. Nearby lay a skip filled with rubbish, no doubt some of the detritus and pieces of broken furniture removed from inside. Amidst the miscellaneous waste, he saw an iron bracket protruding from one side and, limping over, he drew it free before moving back towards the doors. Using the bracket like a crowbar, he succeeded in jemmying one of the doors open. He then edged inside.

Great rents in the ceiling of the theatre let in the gloomy light from outside, allowing Trevor to vaguely see that what grandeur the *SS Berengaria* once possessed was now no more, the interior now resembling a demolished warehouse — something which had all the charm of a dead leper. Every single chair had been removed, along with the drapes and other lavish furnishings, many of them salvaged antique pieces from the cruise ship after which it was named. The floor was a mess of fallen roof beams, smashed tiles, heaps of rubble and discarded waste — the latter no doubt generated by thieves and scavengers who had come in search of trophies to steal. It reminded him of some of the IRA bomb-targeted buildings he had seen.

Two rusting rubbish skips lay near the centre, each filled with detritus. A dead dog, its rat-gnawed remains festering and reeking; three smashed-up fruit machines; a buckled shopping trolley; plastic chairs; and a splintered grand piano lay atop one such pile. The stage area looked as though it had been gutted in some past fire.

An eerie, spine-tingling sound brought his heart to a temporary freeze and raised gooseflesh on his arms. It sounded like a tortured child wailing down a length of corrugated tube; a banshee's drone that conjured up terrifying images.

A bone-chilling wind blasted through the wrecked theatre, raising clouds of dust and grit.

Trevor ran, limping headlong into the darkness. He stumbled over a length of cable before scrambling to his feet. It felt as though his heart was about to burst in his chest.

He had been herded into a shadow-filled corner; he dared not turn round. Tears ran from his bloodshot eyes as he crumpled to his knees. Stricken with fear, he fell into a foetal position and began to gibber.

★   ★   ★

In the rubble-filled bolt-hole, the old man had consumed half of his whisky and his slightly dulled senses allowed some of the pain to ebb away. He was determined to take the painkillers with his last few gulps so that he would be unconscious when he died, but he knew that he would have to wait a while for the alcohol to take full effect, his resilience to the strong liquor having increased during the last three years or so.

However, drink was no longer a means of escape.

The strongbox which had at one time been stuffed with fifty- and twenty-pound notes was empty bar a few coins, testimony to the fact that he was destitute — a broken man, now on the brink of his own self-destruction. Contemplating his downfall, he took another swig from the bottle, the fiery liquid burning his throat.

He hated Morecambe almost to the same degree he despised its inhabitants, and yet it seemed very fitting to him that he had ended up here; for, just like the hotel, he had once been valued and respected. He had enjoyed privilege and been sought out by the elite. Whether due to that thought or the gradual effects of the alcohol, he suddenly decided to explore the decaying hotel — he had not dared try before for fear of something collapsing on him — or even worse, for someone from outside to hear his movements and come and investigate his intrusion or phone the police. Having nothing left to lose, he slowly stumbled his way around the deserted corridors and rooms, peering and using his hands to make out where he was going and avoid tripping over, his battery-powered torch having long, since broken. The building must have been quite a sight, he thought; its architecture was clean and flowing and several of its showpiece rooms still retained the remains of elegant Eric Gill-designed murals and patterned floors. It was a tragedy that something as prized and as grandiose as this had been allowed to fall into such a state.

Shuffling forward, he crept into what had undoubtedly been the main reception hall, its striking murals fading — like him — into obscurity. With a shaking hand, he poured more whisky down his throat, the bottle now nearly empty. Soon it would be time to take a seat, probably on one of the steps of the curved stairway that led to the upper floors, and start pill-munching. Through bleary, bloodshot eyes, he stared into the pitch darkness above him, wondering for a brief moment what it was like up there — wondering if it was just as ruined as the basement and the ground floor. Wondering if it was as ruined as he was.

His mind was drifting now, shadows within the darkness seemingly roving of their own accord. A large rat squeaked and scurried away as he stumbled towards the stairway, his right hand delving into his damp coat pocket for the bag of pills. He had been here before, suicide so tantalisingly close; and, on each occasion, he had lacked the courage to see the act through. Death, it was hoped, would free him from the terrifying realities of life — realities that for so many years he had never, even in his wildest dreams, considered as being rooted in tangible actuality.

Now was the time . . .

That still cogent part of his mind cried out its defiance to the cruel world he had come to hate. Since his arrival in Morecambe he had been persecuted, ostracized, reviled — his sole crime being that he was seen as an outsider; a pariah, an unwelcome visitor amongst these uneducated, ill-informed, insular, northern xenophobes. 'Pervy' — that was what they called him.

Like a leper, he had been forced to endure their bitterness; and yet, if truth be told, he cared nothing for their opinion. From whence the 'Stan' component of his nickname originated, he had no idea.

An unbidden smile creased his lips as a memory of a time some months back came to his drink-addled brain. He had been caught in the act of urinating against the wall of the Morecambe Arndale Centre by a group of schoolboys, not dissimilar to the ones who had tormented him previously, when one of the more educated of their crowd had called him 'Uzbeki!'. Another equally well-educated individual had followed up with a cry of 'Afghani!', demonstrating their scant central Asian geographical knowledge to the full. But the prefix that tended to stick was 'Pervy'.

Through the alcohol-induced fog, he cast his memories back further, to a time just over three years ago when he had been someone else. He raised the bottle, toasting himself; and then, amidst the reminders of glory and with no one else to hear, he said in a clear voice: 'Mandrake Smith. DPhil. Professor of Anthropology. University of Oxford!' His declaration to his former self over, he drunkenly stumbled backwards, managing to catch himself from a fall with an outstretched hand. The titles sounded strange to him now — alien — as if they belonged to another time, another person; and in some sense they did. For he was no longer that self-assured, well respected and — if he was honest — rather pompous eminent scholar who had held a tenure at three internationally renowned universities before accepting an illustrious position at Oxford. He had lectured in São Paulo, New York, Paris, Melbourne . . . the list went on.

Although that said, yesterday, like the day before that and the week — if not the months — before that, he had shuffled alongside the foul-mouthed 'living dead' in a queue at the nearest Late Shop off-licence, waiting to buy his liquor. He had just kept his head down, not once displaying any outward emotion, and yet inside he was seething. *Is this what I've been reduced to?* he thought.

The harsh reality was that he had become a social outcast, an embittered recluse, forced to exist in a world in which his only means of adaptation — and indeed survival — relied on altering his state of consciousness through alcohol. There were a lot of people doing the same in Morecambe. Anti-depressants and cheap booze had become the lifeblood of the town.

Sitting down on a step, he removed the bottle of painkillers and squeezed the lid before unscrewing the cap. Emptying out a handful of the white pills, he stared at them fixedly before chucking them into his mouth. Raising the whisky to his lips, he chased the first dose down, relieved to be cleansing his palette of the sharp taste. He scratched at the grey-white, grizzled beard on his chin and throat before tipping a second lot of pills into his hand. Again he stared at them, memories of his past cruelly assailing his fading consciousness.

Now sixty-two, yet looking a good ten years older, he saw himself as he had been. At fifty-eight, he had been a senior tutor in cultural and social anthropology; a man at the zenith of his academic career. His chosen field had been folklore and primitive religions. His doctoral thesis had been an exploratory investigation into the mechanisms and psychological dynamics behind early belief patterns of various Amazonian, Oceanic and New Guinean autochthones. Adopting a holistic approach, he had set out to evaluate and compare the various religious traditions entrenched within the primordial psyche of such people, with an emphasis on how such belief patterns were reflected in the oral traditions, tribal art and the material culture that underpinned such ideologies. His fieldwork had taken him to the less-explored parts of the world: to the jungles of the Amazon where he had lived amongst the *Waorani* Indians, and to remote villages on the Papua New Guinean mainland and the rainforest, where he had spent the better part of a year amongst the *Gebusi*, the *Bedamini* and the even wilder cannibal indigenes there. He had immersed himself in his work, eager to discover and record every single facet he could about these aboriginal people and their adaptation to both their environment and their incipient contact with colonial powers.

Or had he dreamt it . . . ?

After all, the way he was now, he doubted whether he could cut it as a Big Issue seller.

His lids were drooping as he took another swig from the bottle. He was getting to the stage where he could well be too drunk to carry his act of suicide through. With that thought, he shovelled a further handful of pills into his mouth and began chewing.

What have I become? he thought, melancholy creeping into his dizzying mind as he finished off the dregs in the bottle. His downfall had been brought about by a peculiar chain of events, initiated by the bizarre encounter with an enigmatic man named Thorn, who had walked into his office back in early 2001 and had started to spout the most outrageous claims Smith had ever heard. According to Thorn, a certain Jasper Darkly, manager of a national chocolate manufacturing company, was going to poison vast quantities of Easter eggs in order to murder thousands. Thorn had gone on to suggest that Darkly was intending to offer up a sort of 'blood sacrifice' which would appease a great earth spirit which was already demonstrating its wrath by creating numerous calamities, including such things as mass flooding, mutant births and national subsidence. Only if this entity could be appeased, Thorn had gone on to say, would Britain be saved. He had provided 'evidence' to reinforce his claims, including numerous photographs, satellite images and reports, all of which appeared genuine.

A flicker of a smile came to Smith's lips as he remembered how he had initially dismissed all he had been told. After all, how could anyone sane believe this nonsense — a cult operating under the guise of a chocolate company, blood-thirsty chthonic deities, a rash of severe environmental happenings and goodness knew what else?

However, Thorn had gone further, relating how he worked for a secret government organisation. Time was running out, Thorn had said; and indeed it was, for he was of the opinion that if nothing was done, then Britain was doomed.

Smith found himself unable to counter Thorn's arguments and evidence. The man *was* on to something . . . or *on* something. However, it was indisputable that freak, unseasonable weather was beginning to affect many parts of Britain; why, even many parts of his beloved Oxford were becoming flooded on a regular basis.

But all of that aside, it was the revelation that came later that really got Smith thinking. Thorn had revealed that the only viable means of satiating this unknown entity was to nourish it with the souls of animals. Indeed, that, he claimed, had been the sole reason for his visit — in order to enquire whether, in Smith's learned opinion, animals would suffice.

From Smith's reading on the subject, he knew that many cultures regarded the ritualistic slaying of a person to be of greater symbolic importance than that of an animal; however, he was aware that such substitution could be enacted providing that the numbers were far greater. Thus, for example, five cows or a dozen goats could, to a primitive mind at least, be offered with the same level of religious efficacy as one human. The question therefore was just how on earth Thorn was going to oversee the immolation of what would have to be hundreds of thousands of animals.

'Suffice it to say that such steps are already under way. No doubt you've read about the recent 'outbreaks' of foot-and-mouth?' Thorn had answered, his words still clear in Smith's brain as though spoken only yesterday. That meeting had been the catalyst for the horror that had come later.

Smith broke open another bottle of pain-killers and tipped them into his mouth.

2

Thursday, December 9th, 2004

At seventy-two, Alf Turner was fit and sprightly for a man of his age. He put his reasonably good health down to the fact that he had never smoked and was a firm believer in a brisk forty-minute walk every morning. Although it was still dark outside, he had heard the thunder and the rain all night and he knew it was going to be wet. He zipped up his coat, straightened his glasses and called for Jenny, his ageing black Labrador.

Arthritically, Jenny waddled towards him, her tail wagging.

Leaving his small house, he locked up; and, with Jenny fixed on her lead, set off down the street towards Heysham Village. He had lived in Heysham, the small village neighbouring Morecambe, all of his life, never having ventured abroad or having travelled further afield than Blackpool.

Reaching the end of the street, he took a right turn and crossed the main square, heading for the area down near the so-called 'gatehouse' — an arched building which stood near the old road that lead towards Higher Heysham and Half Moon Bay. From here, he would take the footpath that climbed up the terraced slopes within Vicarage Wood, known locally as Vicar's Wood.

Vicar's Wood was not large; and yet, like the village, it was shrouded in history and superstition. Alf had heard some of this when he had once attended a local history meeting some years back. Stories of strange sightings and witchcraft had abounded not that long ago either, especially after a group of local kids had unearthed the remains of a large dog. Some nutter from Lancaster University had even suggested that the Holy Grail was buried somewhere within, founding his notions on the belief that St. Patrick had somehow got his hands on it and brought it over from Ireland. His theories had been discredited on chronological grounds but they still attracted the odd grail-seeker for whom Glastonbury was too far to travel. Village rumour had it that recently one such eccentric, a well-built South African, had even financed his own — admittedly small-scale — private excavations before mysteriously disappearing.

All of which, not unsurprisingly, was of no real concern to Alf.

Carefully, he climbed the steps up to a higher level of the wood, having to stop every so often so that he could get his breath and give Jenny an encouraging tug. It was muddy underfoot and treacherously slippery, but he was used to walking these woodland paths. He liked the feeling of solitude and stillness up here, the rooftops and chimneys of the village now nestled below him to his right. This, to him, was the real Heysham Village — a small rural enclave within the town proper.

He was now passing a large group of boulders that formed a small rock shelter of sorts, its interior smelling of animal excrement and damp. From here, he set out across an open glade, growths of ferns sprouting on the roughly terraced, ivy-covered ledges that stepped down to the lower ground. The ground itself here was uneven, rabbit holes and small moss-covered rocks making the crossing difficult in the poor light. Over to one side he could see the outline of the so-called 'Druid's Stone' — a lump of roughly rectangular rock, the upper surface of which had been hollowed slightly, whether naturally or artificially, so as to create a slight, trough-like depression. What its purpose was, if indeed it had one, he had never known. It was invariably filled with crushed beer cans and cigarette ends.

Some distance away he heard a car alarm go off, rudely reminding him of how close he still was to the village proper; for right now he was less than two hundred yards from the rear of his local, The Royal Hotel, its rooftop just visible through the foliage. The path now sloped downwards, veering slightly away from the houses on the main street, heading for the ruins of St. Patrick's Chapel.

Exiting the wood, he walked out towards the exposed stretch of headland which sloped down towards the beach. The wind was gusting wildly out here.

Removing his glasses and wiping them dry with a handkerchief, he inhaled, relishing the cold air as it filled his lungs. He put his spectacles back on and saw the distant lights of Grange-over-Sands and Ulverston twinkling across the bay. It was dark, wet, windy, bitterly cold, and the tide was miles out.

Alf reached into a coat pocket for a dog biscuit, which he gave to Jenny. Overhead the sky looked sinister and brooding, the ruins before him silhouetted against the darker sky. These ruins, which he visited almost every day, were remnants from the mid-eighth century A.D. of structures built in order to serve a monastic community, comprising mainly of the small stone chapel, of which only the east wall and the south wall with its arched opening remained. Several steps away from the chapel, at the cliff edge, on a flat, prominent slab of grey rock, were six rock-cut graves. From left to right, as one approached them, the graves became increasingly anthropomorphic, the first one being more or less rectangular in shape whilst that at the other end was far more man-like in outline.

On clear days, the view from up here was exceptional. More so when the early morning sunlight gilded the snow-capped Cumbrian mountains, or when the sun set in a vast cauldron of purples and crimsons on the horizon.

Snout sniffing, Jenny gave a sudden tug and headed for the graves at the cliff edge.

'Steady there, girl!' exclaimed Alf. One wrong step up here and it was a good fifteen-foot drop to the rocks and the ferns on the other side.

Now less than a few steps from the first rock-hewn grave, he could see that there did appear to be something within — a puddle of water, he thought as he approached, the dog continuing to sniff around the edges. Tentatively, he took a step closer, pushing his glasses back on his head as he did so, which enabled him to better focus his vision on just what it was he was looking at. At first glance, it appeared to be nothing more than an old, wrinkled coat resting atop a pool of water; but as his eyes became more accustomed to the darkness, he could see that it was more than that. It was a mucky grey in places, fleshy pink in others. Curious, he bent down.

Alf's face wrinkled in disgust as he continued to stare, trying to make out what exactly it was. It seemed to be semi-solid, like jelly; and like jelly in a mould, it conformed to the dimensions of the rectangular indentation as though it had been forced in. 'What . . . what is that?' he mumbled to himself, eyes widening as something that resembled a flattened hand or a foot became discernible. He was trembling now, sheer horror and absolute disbelief etching his aged features. Was that an ear? That was definitely an eye . . .

Sickened, and yet still not sure just what it was he was looking at, he stood up and backed away. He pulled back further, dragging Jenny with him as though fearful that the gruesome find might spring up and attack. Mumbling confusedly to himself, he looked down and saw a length of twig that he bent to retrieve. Armed with this, he edged forward once more,

Jenny only too eager to accompany him.

Was it a dead animal? The more Alf looked at it, the more it reminded him of something he had once seen on television — one of the *Spitting Image* puppets. That was what it was. It was one of those grotesque, deflated rubber puppets that had been crammed — like a ventriloquist's dummy in a suitcase — into the shallow grave. Was this someone's idea of a joke? Tentatively, he bent and prodded at it, the twig meeting with weak resistance before puncturing the wet flesh. Yellow-red pus and blood dribbled from the wound as he stumbled back in horror.

★   ★   ★

The drumming was becoming louder and louder, skilled hands becoming no more than flashing blurs against stretched hide. It was a chaotic sound; frenzied and . . . to an outsider at least, more than a little unpleasant — threatening, almost. And, as the tempo increased, so too did the level of violence before his eyes.

Flies buzzed around the diminutive man on his right.

By firelight, some twenty men were screaming and tearing at each other with claws fashioned from the razorbills of jungle birds and the teeth of large cats. Blood was streaming from the wounds as the lithe, dark-skinned warriors fought and danced. Three men held another down as two more repeatedly kicked him, laughing their berserkers' glee as their bare feet smacked against exposed flesh. Another man was forcibly hauled around by his topknot of hair before being whirled into a waiting crowd who sprang on him like a pack of wolves, biting and clawing. One unfortunate was getting his genitals twisted and crushed in the fierce grip of another, his eyes turning blood-red with the excruciating pain.

Still the drums beat on, the rhythm intensifying.

With a cry, another crowd of violent men rushed into the fray, their faces painted black. Each brandished a length of stout bamboo with which they began to beat indiscriminately at those already fighting. Some were quickly disarmed and pulled into the thick of the mêlée, whilst those more experienced kept their distance, utilising their weapons to defend as well as attack. It seemed that everywhere, bamboo smacked against skin with bone-jarring impact.

And yet, despite the wanton savagery, there was little suffering. For this was a ritualised display enacted with the sole purpose of 'entertaining' — if one could put it that way — the spectators. This was a demonstration of pain; a visual homage to punished, beaten flesh.

He sat on the dusty ground, watching, cross-legged, eyes wide, taking in every vicious moment with measured indifference, every now and then having to wave a fly away. Several years ago he had seen this rite performed, and he had been shocked and horrified by the seemingly animalistic barbarity he had witnessed. Now it was different, for he had come here with an enlightened mind, a mind no longer slavishly constrained by the academic theories upon which social and cultural anthropology were based. It was what came after, once the bloodshed was over, that he had come to see. Shocking to the Western mind as it was, this act of unparalleled brutality was but the trailer to the main attraction — a warm-up routine; the clowns larking about before the arrival of the lion-tamer.

Soon the fighting was over and the wounded and the dead either limped away or were cleared from the makeshift arena. There had been three fatalities; but in a society that had a very high incidence of violent death, who was counting? Certainly not the tribal elders beside whom he sat. He watched, wincing somewhat as a young man was lifted unceremoniously from the ground, his neck hanging at right angles to his body, clearly broken. Several others, although still alive, were covered in red weals and huge blue-black bruises.

The drumming ceased.

Now that the fighting was over, he turned his attention to the village itself, noting the small collection of ramshackle log-built longhouses with their grey, matted leaf roofs. Each building was relatively low-ceilinged, for none of the villagers stood any higher than his shoulder. Some of the buildings looked to be in an advanced state of decrepitude.

Heaped haphazardly near some of the entrances to the longhouses was a miscellaneous array of mundane goods. Nearby, he could see a large midden formed from dozens of empty Coca-Cola cans, several boxes of Kellogg's Cornflakes, various animal skulls, and what looked like a plane propeller. Over the doorway to one house there hung a thick rope strung with human heads as well as rubber tyres and vehicle registration plates — the incongruity of this macabre welcome bunting striking, and yet not completely out of place. For elsewhere, there were such signs demonstrative of this 'primitive' and 'civilised' assimilation. A rusty motorbike, near to where he sat, had been draped with a pig's skull and ribcage, transforming it into a ghastly hybrid; and, having examined it earlier, he had been slightly amused to discover that a small photograph of Pope John Paul II had been stuck with gum to the inside of the skull. In several of the houses he had been permitted to enter, he had seen small shrines dedicated to the Virgin Mary, and nearly half of the villagers now brazenly displayed large wooden and bone crosses — all further signs that Christianity was beginning to force its insidious and sanctimonious tendrils into the way these people lived and believed.

It had been this knowledge, his awareness that these people were now on the verge of losing their identity and their cultural uniqueness, which had prompted him to sacrifice all of his sabbatical and make the difficult and costly journey out here. If there were answers to the intense turmoil his life was in, he knew that such answers would not be found in any university library or on any psychiatrist's couch. On his previous visit, he had been viewed as one more outsider — an interested nobody who had come here with his own set of preconceptions. Another bloody anthropologist. He had been judged unworthy and unreceptive, unable to fully comprehend the actuality of sorcery and cannibal witchcraft — the *bogay* and the *ogowilil* — on which this particular society was founded.

Now, after his encounter with Thorn, everything was different.

Now, he was ready. Now he was prepared and willing to experience and accept another belief system as being valid. Anthropological theory steadfastly refuted the possibilities that he now knew to be realities, proclaiming instead that the *idea* of magic and religion were but social constructs entrenched within the social group. Accordingly, it was belief alone that maintained the illusion of magical power, nothing more; and, as belief was an unsubstantiated science, it held no academic weight, certainly not amongst his university peers at any rate.

The ground on which he sat with the others was proving uncomfortable; yet he knew better than to stand up, for such an act would be seen as one of great insult. Patiently, he waited, his nerves tingling at the prospect of what he was about to experience, well aware that he alone had been chosen for this particular initiation.

From somewhere over to his left, where fat, ugly-looking swine oinked and squealed from within a crude pen, there came a barely human scream; and moments later a torn and ragged yellow-faced man was dragged out by two others, a halter around his neck. Bloody, dirt-filled bite marks on the prisoner's legs and arms revealed that he had been largely unsuccessful in fending off the voracious hogs; and his left hand had been chewed off completely, ragged bone and torn sinew protruding from the blood-dripping stump.

This was the enemy sorcerer — a practitioner of vile, cannibal witchcraft.

He gulped, eyes continuing to stare, hoping that he would have the courage to see this through; for such things had never, to his knowledge, been seen by any outsider. It was hoped that the bloodshed from minutes before would bolster his resolve; provide him with the strength of will to sit this out. Yet, despite the fact that he had just witnessed some three dozen men beat the living daylights out of each other, he knew that what was forthcoming was going to be something else entirely, something which transcended mere physical violence.

The tribal sorcerer, who was sat on his right, stood up. He was an ugly-looking individual, his limbs elongated, his eyes sunken. His swarthy, withered skin was painted with white and red tribal markings, giving him the macabre appearance of a living, raw skeleton, his face whitened with powder and pigment in order to resemble a skull. Aside from the impressive fan of cassowary feathers he had on his head, what clothing he wore was crude and filthy, fashioned from grim-looking beadwork and black and white striped hide. On his back he carried a strung bow that was almost as long as he was; a quiver containing thirteen black-feathered arrows; and a sling from which a shrunken, hideous-looking infant gawped with hungry eyes and filed teeth. Around both of them, as though their skin had been rubbed in excrement, hovered a thick swarm of flies. The Mickey Mouse wristwatch the sorcerer wore on his left arm looked a tad out of place.

The enemy sorcerer's restrainers unfastened him, eager to do the deed quickly and thus lessen the amount of time they were in direct contact with him. For, despite the fact that his powers had been weakened by the removal of his left hand — the source of his evil — it was clear that they had not been completely nullified. Torn and ragged as he was, the man stood his ground, fixing those before him with malign intent, his muttered maledictions creating a trail of smoke as they left his lips, like that from a fired pistol.

Suddenly, with an ear-splitting screech and hurling curses of his own, the tribal sorcerer bounded forward. With lightning speed he unslung his bow, drew an arrow, notched it and shot, the enemy witch doctor his intended target.

The yellow-faced man dodged and the arrow sped past into the jungle. Yelling his defiance, he began hopping on the spot. Raising his remaining hand, he screamed words at the top of his voice, his bizarre hopping becoming more frenzied. Without his left hand and deprived of his magic tools — his necklace of shrunken heads, his *mojo*-stick, his *wahati* feathers and his *thuti*-parang — he demonstrated that he was still a mighty sorcerer by conjuring images of dread and horror in the minds of the susceptible.

Smith shook as scenes of gory cannibal feasting assaulted his mind. Grisly-faced folk were gnawing on chunks of meat; filthy, grimy hands cracking bones to strip away bloody gobbets and . . .

★   ★   ★

As the nightmare images faded from his mind, consciousness painfully and stealthily crept back.

This wasn't right. Warm sheets and a pillow. The pungent smell of air freshener. The sour taste of whisky lingering in his mouth. The dull throb of a bad hangover pounding at his temples. He opened his eyes to see a dimly lit room — definitely a bedroom, judging by the furniture.

At the sound of his awakening, the door to the bedroom opened and a tall figure entered, stood for a moment observing the sufferer, and walked into his field of vision.

Smith stared at the rather indistinct form — he had lost his glasses a few months ago and had seen no point in getting a new pair, reasoning that Morecambe probably looked better out of focus.

'I must apologise once again, Professor Smith, for interrupting you in your pursuits, but I could not allow such a unique individual as yourself to be lost to us.'

Smith's battered senses were pulling together now, the fog of alcohol fading under the influence of the headache, and he *did* know this man and knew exactly what he wanted to say to him. '*Thorn*! You . . . you . . . ' he stammered. 'You complete and utter bastard! You destroyed me! Why did you have to rob me of my only chance to get out of the nightmare I've inhabited for the past three and a half years?' Coughing violently, he fell back onto the pillow, exhausted by his outburst.

Thorn calmly pulled up a chair next to the bed. 'I didn't realise quite how great my impact was to be when I visited you that day.' He sat down. 'In truth, I thought that you'd probably convince yourself that I had been some crackpot or joker. It was very fortunate that you decided to . . . '

'*Oh, shut up*! Just shut up!' croaked Smith. He sat up and stared about. 'Where are my pills? I'll finish this yet!'

'I've got them.' Thorn rattled a pill container. 'My man saw you buying your painkillers at the chemist and immediately called me for advice. I ordered that he attempt to ensure your survival in whatever way necessary. He was contemplating getting you arrested but then, quite by chance, you were the target of some classic, let's say, Morecambe hospitality.' He saw a measure of comprehension on Smith's face. 'Yes . . . the egg-throwers provided excellent cover and enabled him to switch your painkillers for a harmless placebo. The alcohol did the rest and you were fast asleep when we came down to collect you. Your snoring could wake the dead.'

Smith was watching Thorn with a mixture of hatred and disbelief. 'What do you mean?'

'We've had a base on the upper floors of the hotel for the past couple of weeks now. Just keeping an eye on you, nothing more.'

'Do you mean you've been spying on me?' Smith struggled into a more comfortable position, trying to ignore the protests from his abused body. 'Go away and leave me alone. Can't I even *die* in peace?' Pathetically, he covered his face with his dirty hands and began to sob.

Thorn considered the wreck of a man before him. 'All right. I will leave you alone for a while, if that's what you wish. Long enough to get rid of that hangover anyway. You can't leave this set of rooms but there's a bathroom over there and food on the table. There's some clean clothes in the wardrobe. I hope they fit. I would also suggest that you at least make use of the bath. You stink.' He got up. 'It may be a cliché, but your country needs you.' With those words, he shut the door and Smith heard the key turn in the lock.

3

Friday, December 10th, 2004

Heysham's ugliest and fattest man, 'Big' Barry Crowley, lived with his hag of a mother in a semi-detached bungalow. In addition to his gross appearance, obscene personal hygiene and unappealing demeanour, he was also more than a little addled in the brain, partly as a consequence of what he did for a living. He loved no one but himself, his German Shepherd dog, 'Killa', and his mother, although he did love Fridays; for every Friday morning it was his job to sample the chemical storage tanks at work. Clandestinely, he would siphon off a little benzene, or whatever else was going into an empty bottle, for himself and his dear mother — not to drink or inhale, but rather to add to the bath water. It produced lovely, multicoloured bubbles that he and his mother would stare at for hours. It also did things for the skin.

Barry had worked at the relatively small solvent recycling plant on the road between Heysham and Middleton for the past thirteen years. The conditions there were absolutely horrendous — what with the terrible, lachrymatory stink and the early mornings, not to mention the hazardous nature of the job. It was an environment of barely breathable caustic fumes; a glue-sniffer's paradise; an environmentalist's hell.

Yesterday, Barry had celebrated his thirty-seventh birthday — which, by a strange coincidence, was one year for every stone he currently weighed — by indulging in two of his favourite pastimes: eating and getting wasted on drink. As was only natural on his birthday, he had phoned in sick, citing the usual ailment of a bad back. 'But, boss . . . I'm stuck in me bed. I can't get up . . . Ohhh! The pain . . . it's intolerable. I might see about givin' doctor a ring,' he had lied, not really caring whether his boss would fall for the lame deception or not.

Barry's drinking exploits around Morecambe and Heysham bordered on the legendary, his pastime largely funded by his imbecilic mother. Whenever he 'took time off', it was not unusual for him to quite easily drink his way through anything up to twenty-five pints in an afternoon. 'Mouthwash. Nowt but mouthwash,' he would comment, to the alarm and astonishment of those watching, his many empty pint glasses left standing on the table before him in tribute to his drinking ability.

And by God could he eat! On a typical binge he would polish off at least three portions of fish and chips. 'Just a little summat to soak up the beer,' he would add, brazenly patting his wobbling gut. Sometimes he would devour an entire family-sized portion of fried chicken nuggets and chips — the so-called 'Bargain Bucket' — on the rear steps to the Pleasureland Arcade, sitting like a cartoon grizzly bear, a glower on his face as he munched and stared aggressively back at curious passers-by. If in Heysham, where his takeaway options were much more limited, he would probably have to settle for some more chips and a few steak and kidney puddings from the chip shop.

Yesterday, however, things had been a little different.

For there he had been, quite the thing, sitting at the bar in The Royal Hotel in Heysham Village, drinking away and celebrating his birthday with a huge plate of chips at his elbow, when some old codger had walked in, his face as white as chalk. 'Looks like you've seen a ghost, mate,' Barry had commented, dunking a fat chip into a bowl of tomato sauce.

'Could be that I have,' the pensioner had mumbled before ordering himself a large brandy.

Barry had listened in on the conversation the old man had had with the barman, something to do with how he had been out with his dog and had found what he thought was a corpse lying in one of the graves up in the ruins. Well, needless to say, the barman and another couple of locals had made a few passing comments about their informer's state of mind, telling him that he should lay off the bottle and get more fresh air. But the old geezer had been damn persistent and

55

the more Barry had listened in, the more the tale had piqued his morbid curiosity. There were discussions about getting the police involved, and then somebody suggested a reporter pal of his who worked for *The Visitor* — the weekly Morecambe newspaper.

'Alf, what kind o' body were it?' a man smoking a pipe had inquired, clearly unbothered about the smoking ban.

'It were the ugliest thing ye could imagine, Derrick. It were 'orrible, all shrivelled or somethin' . . . like a slug sprinkled wi' salt.'

'*Oi*! I'm eatin' 'ere,' Barry had complained, having just added salt to his chips.

Visibly shaking, Alf took a large gulp of brandy. 'It were like somethin' straight out o' a Hammer horror film. I've sat at home wi' the doors bolted all mornin' not knowing what to do. Missed ma doctor's appointment an' all. Do you think I should phone the police?'

Another old codger looked up from where he sat at the far end of the bar doing a crossword, a fag in his mouth. 'Well that's the problem, ain't it? Seein' as you discovered it, you'd be the first suspect. It's always the way. I've watched *Murder She Wrote* an' *Taggart* an' I know how these detectives an' folk think. It's a minimum o' fifteen years fer murder. Take my advice an' say nothin'.' His caution over, he returned to his puzzle. Six down had him vexed.

Alf ignored his drinking buddy. 'What should we do?'

The cheery grin on the barman's face melted away. 'You're serious about this, Alf, aren't you?'

'I'm tellin' you straight. There's a dead body up there!'

Barry snorted indignantly. 'I'll go up an' 'ave a butcher's.' Being the youngest and by far the biggest, he saw it as his duty to go and sort out the problem. Besides, he wanted to have a look for himself, having never seen a real dead body before. Grabbing a fistful of chips, he stood up. Cramming his chips into his mouth, he left The Royal Hotel and started his slow and laborious plod up to the ruins, passing the picturesque, Saxon-built Church of St. Peter's on his right. He had the gait of a pregnant

57

walrus and despite the fact that a normal, healthy individual could do the walk in less than five minutes, it took Barry the best part of a quarter of an hour to reach his destination.

Twenty minutes later he was back in The Royal Hotel.

'Well?' a host of interested voices had asked.

'There were nowt there.' Barry looked at Alf.

'Nothin'?' Alf had asked. 'There was nothin' there?'

All of that had been yesterday.

This morning, Barry was getting ready for work. He checked his watch, realising that it had just gone six; and farting uproariously, loud enough to wake the neighbours, he slumped out of bed. He never bothered with breakfast, not even a slice of toast or a cup of tea. That said, in his lunch bag, his mother had made him up an entire loaf's worth of sandwiches, all with various filings. Fried egg and mushy peas was his favourite.

Getting his specially reinforced bike from the back shed, he secured his lunch bag to it and set off. It was just over two miles to where he worked and at his slow cycling rate it normally took him the best part of twenty minutes to get there. He made a comical sight, his fat backside bulging over the sides of the straining saddle as he panted and puffed his way to work.

It was another cold and dark morning.

Shivering in the chill and the light drizzle, Barry pedalled on. Passing The Old Hall pub and the Heysham health centre on his right, he continued along Heysham Road.

Aside from the two nuclear power stations, the chemical plant where he worked was one of the largest employers in the immediate area. Both power stations were fast reaching their decommissioning phase, there being but a skeleton staff there now, and when they closed down it would assuredly swell the ranks of the unemployed masses who currently inhabited the area.

The chemical plant where Barry worked loomed on the horizon, its perimeter fenced with metal railings topped with razor wire to keep out trespassers, although no one in their right mind would wish to sneak inside. By day and by night the place stank — more so at night when black, toxic, cloud-like discharges were expelled under cover of darkness. The noisome, gaseous by-products of the solvent recycling process polluted the very air and killed plant life. Despite the repugnant odours and potentially hazardous fallout from the plant, directly across from it, on the other side of the road, there was a small caravan park which mostly provided for the elderly and the desperate; and on more than one occasion, the shocked residents had awoken to discover the ground littered with dead birds and their windows coated in a mysterious and very unpleasant sooty residue.

Barry was slogging towards a railway bridge when a sudden sound chilled him to the very marrow. It was a long drawn-out wail — a howl of pure evil, a nightmarish ululation.

'What the . . . ?' he asked out loud as he brought the bike to an abrupt halt, eyes staring into the pre-dawn darkness.

He waited, his overworked heart pounding in his heaving chest.

Now that the initial shock was wearing off, he began to go through the short list of logical explanations. Could it have been a siren from the power stations, somehow warped and carried on the wind, perhaps alerting the sleeping residents of Heysham to an imminent massive radioactive leak or a reactor core meltdown? Nah, he thought, shivering. It had been much closer, for a start. So Lancashire's Chernobyl was postponed for another day.

He was just about to set off, consigning the weird noise to perhaps an anomalous bird call, when he caught sight of movement in the bushes down by the railway embankment. Peering, he thought he made out a small figure, possibly a child, turn and run into the tunnel below.

A horn blared shortly before a car sped past from behind, causing Barry to jump as well as alert him to the fact that he was still on the main road.

'Bog off!' he shouted, sticking two fingers up at the dwindling red tail lights.

It was probably just one of his workmates. He clambered off his bike and went to the bridge parapet. Throwing his gaze into the shadows of the tunnel mouth, he thought he could make out the small shape now sat on the rails. The silhouette of a pale face, which in the poor light looked somehow crumpled, stared back at him.

The figure beckoned him before crawling into the darkness. A luminous green mist trailed behind it.

Contrary to what a lot of people thought about Barry, and despite his solvent-abused brain, he was reasonably intelligent. With no brothers or sisters and no 'true' friends, he had grown up occupying much of his time with reading. One of his main interests had always been the paranormal and, on the stage of his largely puerile and decidedly strange imagination, *he* was the charismatic investigator who explored the supernatural — hence, his eventual willingness to go and ascertain the presence or absence of a certain corpse yesterday up at the ruins. This same interest made him clamber over the small fence and begin the downward struggle towards the tunnel mouth.

★   ★   ★

Smith had stared hard at his reflection for a full twenty minutes through the stylish, new, horn-rimmed spectacles that he had been given. He had taken Thorn's advice of the night before and bathed, washing away most of the grime and the stink which had impregnated his skin over the past many months of rough living; and now he stood, preparing to shave away the short, scruffy beard he had grown. His gaze hardened the longer he stared at and *into* the mirror, questions forming in his mind, hoping perhaps that his reflected double could provide the answers. There was much bitterness and confusion recorded in his slate grey eyes, and each line on his whisky-cracked face seemed to stand for something more poignant than a few years of alcohol abuse.

The image that stared back at him was not the man he would have predicted he would become. Nevertheless, he was now the man that fate — that strange and inexorable path to death — had decreed he would be. With that thought, a resolution came to him and he broke free from his own mesmerising gaze.

There was a generous assortment of toiletries on hand and the bathroom suite itself was, like the bedroom, of a high quality, quite luxurious actually. Somehow, Thorn had ensured that the bathroom was provided with both hot and cold running water. Reaching for the shaving foam, he sprayed some into his hand and applied it liberally to his scruffy beard. He was initially hesitant about using a razor, but soon got back into the hang of it; and slowly, without any nicks, he scraped the fuzz of grey-white hair away.

Now that the beard was gone, he felt a surprising wave of vulnerability course through him, almost as though his mask had now been removed and he was recognisable once more. His disappearance from Oxford at the end of Hilary Term back in 2001 had been kept relatively low-key, yet had still attracted the attention of at least two national tabloid newspapers. Rumours had abounded that he had perished out on one of his field trips, only for later claims to arise that he had been sighted in north Oxford.

It was true that he had been abroad — he had spent three months in Papua New Guinea on sabbatical — but his college, St John's, had always assumed he would return to his usual routine. However, armed with the knowledge that he now possessed and haunted by the visions of what he had witnessed, he had been unable to resume his academic pursuits. The university had been somewhat sympathetic, keen not to relinquish its rapacious grasp on one of his outstanding accomplishments, yet they had no idea of the demons he was fighting within himself. Smith had almost laughed when the dean of his college had suggested stress counselling. The offers of increased pay and fewer teaching duties had been similarly dismissed and, finally, he had sold his house, closed the door on his office and simply walked away from it all.

The memory of that moment of perfect

clarity was still fresh in his mind. The weight of pretence had been lifted, and for a few weeks he had felt younger and more liberated than in the previous twenty-five years. With his newfound freedom he had even managed to shake off the nightmares for a while.

However, it had been a brief respite from the horror and paranoia. Like most things, that time had ended violently. One night he had been drinking in a cheap rented room somewhere on the outskirts of Oldham when a twisted face had appeared at the third floor window. Bloodstained and screaming, the vision had terrified him as he recognised the cannibal shaman who had so contributed to his own enlightenment. He had reacted instinctively and punched at the face, belatedly realising it was the window he hit. He had been inches away from severing his wrist.

That memory was as raw as ever, but he was able to recover more quickly these days. He dried his naked face and dressed in the clothes that had been provided. They were fairly nondescript, though a hundred times better than his recent attire.

A key turned in the lock and a young man rather hesitantly entered the room carrying a breakfast tray, which he tried to set down quickly and leave.

Smith grabbed his arm and pulled the stranger towards him. 'Don't go running off now. I would like the pleasure of your boss's company. Tell him he can lock the door but I only stay of my own volition.'

'I think Mr. Thorn is hoping to see you after breakfast, sir. I could ask him to join you, if you like.'

Smith stared aggressively into the young man's eyes. He then dismissed the flunky with a wave of his hand. Some habits from his Oxford days died hard and an instinctive dislike of the young was one of them. It was mostly bravado on his part; but he knew that he would need to be assertive in this strange situation, so he may as well begin now. He started on his breakfast.

About ten minutes later Thorn appeared, a cup of coffee in one hand and a bulky folder in the other. 'Ah, all rested I hope? We've a lot to discuss and the sooner we get the recriminations out of the way, the sooner we can get down to business.'

He sat on the edge of the bed and drew a table closer. 'So please, go ahead.'

Now that Thorn was actually prepared to listen, Smith felt unsure how to proceed. Certainly, he blamed this man for the spectacular collapse of his life and he had wanted to find him on many occasions — to rail at him, demand reparation, or just beat him up and possibly kill him. Now, however, after a relatively sumptuous breakfast of mackerel fillets, scrambled eggs, sausages and toast, he decided, temporarily at least, to rein in his lust for revenge. God alone knew how many times he had chewed everything over in his plagued mind. And, he had to admit, just as there had been times when he could quite easily have murdered this man, providing he had been given the opportunity, there had also been times when he had been forced to think along different lines. After all, was it really Thorn's fault that he had been unable to cope with the realisation that all of his life's work and academic belief had been based on an almighty misapprehension? It could be argued that Thorn had illuminated him to the hidden reality. He put his cup of tea down and ran a hand across his smooth chin. 'We'll get to the recriminations later, Thorn, and believe me there *will* be a reckoning.' He sat back in the armchair and crossed his legs. 'But for now, just tell me what national disaster you've uncovered this time.'

If Smith's tone was a little sarcastic, Thorn took his words at face value. 'Excellent,' he beamed. 'I was convinced that you were the one I needed for this problem.' He opened the folder, removed a sheaf of papers and spread them over the table. Unlike the collection of warped pictures he had shown the ex-professor back in early 2001, these were a mixture of maps, newspaper cuttings, photographs of monuments and vandalised walls covered in graffiti and even a couple of *Welcome to Morecambe* tourist leaflets. Taking two Polaroids from the pile, he slung them over to where Smith sat. 'What do you make of these?' he asked.

Both photographs showed scrawled graffiti.

The lettering stood out like a splash of arterial blood on a dark grey background in sloppy, crimson words. Smith's lips puckered and a frown creased his forehead as he studied them, realising that he had seen graffiti like this elsewhere:

PREPARE
FOR HE IS COMING

'Now I know this looks odd, but believe me it all connects, at least I hope to God it does.' Thorn looked intently at his sceptical audience of one. 'I know that last time I told you both too much and too little — for that I apologise. I underestimated you. This time I need a partner, not just an opinion. Thus, I think you've the right to know everything I do. There's reason to believe that some ritualistic murders have taken place.'

Smith was still looking at the photographs, wondering if Thorn had lost his mind as he himself had. *What was this nonsense?* And, more to the point, knowing Thorn, where was it going to take him? Was this another embarkation point for the world of madness? He looked up. 'Four questions,' he said abruptly, wanting to seize the initiative before this encounter descended further into absurdity. 'Question one — what's your full name? Question two — who exactly do you work for? Question three, and please ask for an extra sheet of paper should you need it — just how closely have you been following me all these years? And, question four — just why the hell *should* I help you?'

'You've got questions. I'll provide you with . . . the answers. My name was originally Sebastian Maximilian D'arcy, but I changed it to Robert Thorn. I figured it looked better on a CV. Less Etonian. Anyway, most people call me 'Thorn'. Your second question is a little more difficult to answer. When we first met I told you that I worked for a government agency, which was true, but I didn't specify which government. The organisation I work for is called the Hapsburg Foundation and was set up in the 1920s following the Federal investigations in a town in the U.S. called Innsmouth.' Thorn took a sip from his coffee before continuing. 'As to how closely I've been following you, well, that again is a hard one to answer — for you've not been altogether easy to follow. Let's just say that we tracked you to Lancashire at the beginning of October. It was quite by chance that one of my men saw you sitting on a bench outside the Morrisons store. However, please don't think that you've been under twenty-four hour surveillance or anything like that. To answer your final question, if . . . '

'If what?'

'Well, if you assist me, then I'll help you.'

'Oh, yeah? How? Are you going to get me my job back or set me up with a villa in Sri Lanka? Maybe throw in a swimming pool or a fast car . . . '

'I can get you back to Papua New Guinea.'

'You . . . you can?'

'It's what you want, isn't it? A chance to exorcise your demons and free yourself from the nightmares? Well, isn't it?'

So this was Thorn's solid gold bargaining chip. There was little Smith could do but go along with things for the time being; and that in itself only angered him further, knowing that he was, at least to some extent, at this man's mercy. 'And these?' Derisively, he held up the photographs.

'Well, as you can probably tell, both photographs were taken using a flash. The strange thing is that the graffiti only appears for a few hours and is only visible during the hours of darkness. There's no trace of spray paint or anything else come morning light to even suggest that the writing was ever there.'

'*So?* What makes you think that this is related to these . . . murders you're on about?'

Thorn smiled coldly. 'Well, it would appear that something similar happens to the bodies.'

* * *

Veronica Crowley got the call at a quarter to ten that morning, informing her that her son Barry had been 'found' — not that he had ever really been lost — and that she had better get herself ready to come down to the Morecambe police station to help out in their 'inquiries', as they had put it. At sixty-eight, in poor physical health, and with the mental age of a ten-year-old, she had found it all very trying; but nevertheless she had somehow fixed her curlers and flung on her dressing gown and a pair of slippers, worried and yet also strangely pleased to be doing something different from her usual humdrum life. 'I'm goin' to help the police,' she had bragged to her neighbour as she waited outside in the rain for the police car. 'They say that our Barry's in trouble or somethin'.'

On arrival at the police station some twenty-five minutes later she had been ushered inside like a wanted criminal, the few officers on duty regarding her with bemused looks.

'Mrs. Crowley, I'm sergeant Mick Humphreys, and I was just hoping that you could — ' started the policeman who was guiding her.

'What's wrong wi' our Barry? Where is he?' Without her false teeth, Veronica's interruption was spat, rather than spoken, in a wet slather.

'He's . . . he's asked for you.'

'Ye what?'

'Just keep calm, please, Mrs. Crowley.' Sergeant Humphreys had been part of the Morecambe and Lancaster constabulary for the best part of twenty years, and as a consequence he thought he had encountered virtually every kind of person known to man. This, however, was something he had never had to deal with. Stopping at a cell, he signalled over the warden. 'This is purely for . . . ' He was about to say 'his own protection'; but, looking at the old woman and obviously aware that she was mentally handicapped in some way, he just coughed and signalled for the door to be unlocked.

The heavy door was opened.

In the centre of the cell sat Barry, cross-legged, as naked as a newborn. His flabby frame was torn and ragged, unsightly slabs of flesh hanging in teeth-marked loops like stretched crimson putty from his fat upper body. Man boobs sagged like veiny, water-filled balloons, ready to burst. Arms like huge, puffy pink sausages were uncomfortably restrained behind his back. There was a pervasive odour of dead fish about him as though he had spent the morning skinning squid. Tears poured from his bloodshot eyes as he looked up. 'Mutha . . . ' he slurred, bile-like drool dribbling from his mouth. In addition to the fact that his flesh had become discoloured, having now taken on a nauseous, greenish tinge, there was little doubt that whatever had happened to him had rendered him incurably mad.

★   ★   ★

Later that evening Smith sat sipping his tea, studying some of the paperwork Thorn had gathered, ideas forming in his mind. The horrors of his past, coupled with the acute alcoholism, had undoubtedly removed, or at the very least dulled, much of his intellectual focus, compounding the difficulty he was having with trawling through the enigma he had been presented with. Nonetheless, he had largely stuck with it, spending much of the day delving further into the madness. He glanced at the watch Thorn had given him, noticing that it was already now half-past ten in the evening. He would retire to his bed soon, aware that Thorn had suggested that they go for a drive out early the next morning. Apparently there was something that Thorn wanted to show him.

His room door remained locked. Thorn obviously had no desire as yet to let him go free — not that there was anywhere he could go. He had no money left and no means of transport.

Resignedly, Smith turned his attention back to the documents, a notepad with what he presumed was Thorn's handwriting catching his eye yet again. On it was written:

MORECAMBE —

Current Hapsburg Foundation Rating 6.24 indicates a 38.5% increase in supernatural activity over the last year.

High preponderance of unexplained phenomena, ranging from apparition sightings to UFO possibilities.

Unprecedented level of social/architectural declivity not intrinsically supported by North-South economic division.

Grail connections?

Recent Chinese cockler deaths — possible death cult activity/sacrifice not as yet ruled out.

Dagon? Mother Hydra? Great Cthulhu?

Approx. geometric centre of UK. Next to this was an image of Britain and

Ireland circumscribed by a circle drawn in pencil. The compass point used to do this went through Morecambe.

Heysham Head — Mesolithic Site Excavated 1992. Missing archaeologist(s)? Ask Edward!

Pre-Christian Burials. Unexcavated Tumuli. Area known as 'The Barrows'.

Labyrinth Petroglyph.

Witchcraft connections with nearby Vicarage Wood.

Mood levels among populace — despondent (borderline critical).

Reference to strange statue found in Saqqara (Egypt) — cf. Item in store 33. #1107.

Full name derivative/toponymic etymology unknown. Bay of Death?

Interesting comparison in words with *mor* beginning (eg. morgue, moribund, mortuary etc.) <u>MORRIGAN</u>!

<u>Morrisons?</u>

4

Saturday, December 11th, 2004

At half-past eight in the morning Smith and Thorn slipped out of the rear exit of the Midland Hotel and made their way onto the promenade. The weather was surprisingly fine this morning with a crisp, fresh breeze gusting in from across the bay, carrying with it the strong tang of salt. Because of this, Thorn had suggested over breakfast that they actually walk to their destination, rather than take the car, which he had parked nearby.

'Last night you mentioned you had seen the mysterious graffiti elsewhere,' said Thorn.

Smith nodded. 'Come on, I'll show you. It might not be exactly the same, but it certainly looked similar.' With that, he thrust his hands into the smart new coat he had been given, his scarf already fastened snugly around his neck. It was obvious that most of this gear had not come from any of the countless Morecambe charity shops.

Together they crossed the road and made for the covered walkway. The Woolworths store and the cheap amusement arcade that stood on either side were closed, large metal shuttering down over the latter.

'It's on the wall just up here,' commented Smith.

They entered the tunnel and took several steps inside.

'There!' Smith pointed.

'I don't see it.'

'But it's . . . ' Smith stopped. 'Are you sure?'

Thorn ran a hand down the board, it being nothing more than a deep blue painted wooden panel. Despite his own, albeit limited, psychic powers, he could feel nothing out of the ordinary. 'Nothing. Just wood.'

Smith could see it. It still looked wet and glistening. He reached out, fingers tracing the lettering. 'I can see it, Thorn. *It's there!*'

Thorn took a step back. 'Fine. In fact, I was rather hoping that you would be able to.' He nodded knowingly to himself.

Smith was eager to ask more about this anomaly, but Thorn's smug look irked him and he changed the subject. 'So where are we going now?'

'Heysham Village.' Thorn cupped a hand, lit a cigarette and took a draw. 'It's three miles or so from here.'

'I can't walk that far! For your information, I'm a physical wreck. I certainly won't be able to walk back. My legs aren't up to it.'

'Don't worry, the village has a reliable bus service. Tell you what, just to sweeten the deal, I'll also get lunch. The Royal Hotel does a good steak and kidney pie.'

'You're going to have to. I'm broke.' Smith held out his hands, palms upwards as though to emphasise the point. 'I've got nothing.' It was a blatant and painful statement of fact.

Thorn merely smiled and headed for the alley's exit.

'Don't you walk away while I'm talking to you! *I said, I've got nothing*! And you're to blame.' The entrenched rage that had been allowed to fester unchecked within Smith boiled to the surface, his cheeks flushing red. He came to an abrupt halt, stubbornly refusing to go any further, and pointed to himself. '*You* did this, Thorn! *You* . . . corrupted me. You're responsible for all that I've lost and all that I've now become.'

'You know that's not true.' Thorn threw his still-smoking cigarette to the ground. 'It was not *I* who told you to go back to Papua New Guinea. Indeed, had I known that was where you planned to go, I would have done my best to try and dissuade you. I know what you experienced out there.' He gave a sly, almost cruel smile. 'It's because you *did*, that I now have need of you.'

Smith cursed under his breath. 'So just where are we going?'

'I've told you. Heysham Village. The ruins up on Heysham Head to be precise. It's about an hour's walk from here, so it will give us time to go over some of the ideas you may have. I don't suppose you've been there, have you?'

'I never ventured that far.' Smith took stock of his reply. His answer seemed ironic, considering he had travelled to so many distant and exotic places; and yet now he went no further than the nearest off-licence. Indeed, for the past eighteen months his life had been condensed to less than a dreary square mile. The more he thought about it, the more it seemed to ring true for many of the locals he had seen and overheard. As a professional anthropologist, it had not taken him long to notice a strong xenophobic and reluctant attitude to travel amongst many of those he had encountered. There was a very real and prevalent Morecambe 'mindset' which he had observed — a psychological numbing; a strong sense of inertia which perpetuated the masses in not advancing or improving — be it by travel or inflated life experience — the socio-geographical lot which they had been allocated. The majority seemed morose and unwilling to embrace change; content almost to wallow in their pervasive, impoverished despair. Sure, they had their drink and their cheap thrills, maybe a game of Bingo or a bit of line-dancing once a week; but that aside, most of them seemed slaves to Morecambe's siren's song of the dull, the unimaginative and the familiar; the same old places and the same old faces. Most seemed to be waiting to die in this largely gerontocratic dump. *Was the same thing happening to him? Had he become similarly . . . infected?*

Crossing the road, they passed the War Memorial and rejoined the promenade.

There were a few people out and about. On separate occasions two joggers overtook them and an elderly man walking a scraggy-looking dog gave them a brusque nod of his head. The tide was at least two miles out and several bait-diggers could been seen on the sands with their parked trailer, making the most of the fair weather.

'Well, any ideas about the photographs?' Thorn asked, keen to cut the ice somehow.

'A few.' Smith stole his gaze away from the tall, rusting Polo Tower, a remnant of what had once been Morecambe's fairground. Aside from the two photographs he had initially studied, there had been others; equally inexplicable acts of 'profane' — if indeed that was what they were — vandalism. He turned his gaze to his right, his eyes narrowing, and looked out at the expanse of coast, the words *'Prepare, for He is coming'* going through his brain. What did it mean? Did it mean anything, or was it just pure gibberish? Who exactly was this *He?*

It was obvious to Thorn that Smith was not yet being fully co-operative. 'Some view, isn't it?' he asked, following the older man's gaze.

'Is it?' Sullenly, Smith swung his gaze inland once again. The scenic contrast could not have been more striking. On his right — arguably one of the best views in Britain. On his left — certainly a contender for one of the worst. It seemed to him as though a faint sickly-red haze, like a pall of industrial smog-like pollution, hung over the very town.

Virtually the whole of the Morecambe front they were now passing on their left was one big waste ground, the fairground having long since been demolished and never re-built. Throughout most of the 1980s, Frontierland, as it had been called, had been a reasonable attraction; certainly not on a par with Blackpool's Pleasure Beach, but still a worthy visit for families and those on holiday. It had had the usual rides and had been prestigiously opened with all the razzmatazz that the council could afford by one Jeremy Beadle — the 'prankster-star' of such Saturday evening entertainment as the unmissable *Game for a Laugh* and *You've Been Framed*. It had served the local children well, offering them a level of escapism from their banal lives hitherto denied in a place which catered little for those not interested in Bingo or drinking themselves to oblivion.

A wry smile creased Thorn's mouth as he too stared towards the dereliction. He pointed at a ramshackle, garishly painted boat-like structure. 'You see that? Over there, atop that mountain of rubble . . . Noah's Ark. All that now remains of Morecambe's fairground . . . that eyesore of a tower aside. Rather . . . symbolic, don't you think? An Old Testament relic left floating on a sea of destruction. I remember receiving a photograph of it some months back and thinking to myself how well it seemed to *encapsulate* this town's demise.'

Smith's mind was elsewhere, still cogitating over the images he had seen the day before and the notes Thorn had jotted down in his notebook. From what he remembered, the Morrigan had been a Celtic mother goddess — a mythological being venerated in several aspects, one being a goddess of war and sorcery. Some myths described her as being tripartite in the sense that she had been formed from, or at least could assume, three different manifestations or representations. What all the other references were about, he had no idea. The Egyptian connection certainly had him puzzled. To hell with Noah's Ark; it was time to ask something a bit more pertinent. 'Thorn, your notes make reference to an object from Egypt and its possible relationship to all of this. Tell me more.'

'You mean item number one thousand, one hundred and seven in store thirty-three,' Thorn replied guardedly yet precisely. 'It's a small ivory figurine from a temple votive cache in Saqqara, the western location of the Memphite necropolis. Although its exact provenance is unknown, in fact it turned up on the black market about twenty years ago; I and others are certain of its authenticity. It dates to the First Dynasty, probably unearthed from one of Professor Emery's digs in the late 1930s, and is unusual in the sense that it would appear to bear an uncanny resemblance to the deceased comedian, Eric Morecambe. Glasses, funny stance and all.'

'*What?* You're having me on!' Smith almost choked.

'I wish I was. But no, there is a similarity.' Thorn hesitated before reaching into a jacket pocket and taking out a small notebook. From within its pages, he removed a small passport-sized photograph. 'Here. Have a look for yourself.'

Smith took the photo and stared at the grainy image, eyes widening in recognition. '*Christ!* I see what you mean.' He handed it back, reluctant to examine the anachronistic image too closely. There *was* something deeply unsettling about it — it was almost as though he expected it to suddenly start singing 'Bring me Sunshine'. For it to say something along the lines of, *'Well, what do you think of Morecambe so far?'* Then, with a wiggle of the glasses on its face — if indeed that was what they were — it would say, *'Rubbish!'*

There was a slightly larger-than-life-sized bronze statue of the town's 'favourite son' — 'Our Eric' — not half a mile from where they were.

'You think that's weird? You haven't heard or seen anything yet.' Thorn took a puff from his newly lit cigarette. 'Although I'm fairly sure that much is included in the notes, I think I should just fill you in a bit more on some of the background. Just over a month ago, after Halloween, it came to my attention that there was something supernatural about to take place in this area. Now, normally I don't bother myself with trivial occult gatherings or anything as relatively harmless as the odd black mass, but there was something about the details regarding this event that caused those who still remain loyal to my organisation to sit up. A detectable paranormal shift took place here recently.' His eyes narrowed as he gazed towards the area of seafront known as The Battery. 'Though where exactly, we don't know.'

Smith was only half-listening, the thought that a five-thousand-year-old Egyptian artefact could in some way be linked to Eric Morecambe causing his mind to spin. The statue was unmistakably Egyptian, both in dress and artistic style, and presumably would have been passed off as 'a bit unusual' at the time of its discovery. However, to anyone who knew of Eric Morecambe — who himself would have been only a boy at the time of the statue's discovery — the resemblance was uncanny.

'A bizarre little find, don't you think?' inquired Thorn, noting the perplexed look on his associate's face.

'Very. Makes you wonder what Professor Emery himself would have made of it. You know, come to think of it, Emery looked a bit like Eric Morecambe.' Smith loosened his scarf a little. They were now approaching the limit of his local geographical knowledge, venturing into foreign parts far — almost a mile — from his run-down sanctuary. Once again, that very thought made him think of just how insular and frightened — if that was how it could be described — he had become. He turned his head and gazed back at the forlorn sight of the Midland Hotel, wondering briefly if he would ever see it again.

They turned a bend in the promenade and the derelict hotel vanished from sight, houses now blocking it from view.

Before them lay a mile-and-a-half stretch of promenade, the sloping head-land at Heysham Head visible some mile further. A green swathe of land could be seen running down to a twenty-foot or so high cliff edge, the uppermost grey corner of Heysham One nuclear power station's reactor building visible just beyond.

'That's it,' said Thorn, pointing.

Smith paused, reluctant to go one step further. A sudden cold shiver through his body reminded him he needed a drink.

Force of habit made him reach into his coat pocket with his right hand, searching for a bottle that was not there. He looked to where his companion pointed, his heart sinking both as a result of having no whisky and at the walk ahead of them.

'Are you all right?'

Smith took a few shallow breaths. He knew that with each step, he was now venturing into the unknown. Goodness knew how many people walked along this stretch of promenade every day, yet for him it was as though each step was now being taken on a hostile, distant planet.

There was nobody else to be seen; even the bait-diggers had vanished from view.

Now having passed the area known locally as The Battery, they were venturing into Heysham. The buildings they could see were drab and fairly nondescript, the rear-facing sides of barber shops and premises selling fishing tackle and other odds and ends. It was a bleak, built-up landscape, interspersed with the occasional patch of rubble indicative of where a block of housing or B&B had been torn down to make way for something better — a something better that was yet to appear, and in all likelihood would not for several years, if at all.

Smith found himself reflecting that *anyone* could hide out here, grow a beard — or shave one, in the case of Osama Bin Laden — and become indistinguishable from the indigenous population. Lord Lucan, the *real* Saddam Hussein, and numerous Serbian war criminals were no doubt sat in upstairs rooms watching on battered televisions the world's futile attempts to track them down.

This was indeed such an environment. After all, he had lived here for over a year and a half and no one had ever asked him his name.

A dull ache in Smith's legs alerted him to the fact that this was probably as far as he had walked in many a year. 'This had better be worth it, Thorn,' he moaned.

'I'm hoping it will be. It'll be a wasted morning otherwise.' Thorn turned his gaze towards the drab houses. 'Hardly your city of dreaming spires, is it?'

Smith gave Thorn's question scant

attention. It was perfectly clear that this was not Oxford. Even the slummiest parts of Oxford, notably Cowley and the Blackbird Leys estate, were not as bad as this. *Scheming liars*, maybe, he thought. Yes, the town of 'scheming liars' — that had a certain ring to it.

'Would you care for a cigarette?' asked Thorn.

'Yes.'

Thorn removed a cigarette from his packet, lit it and handed it over.

Smith eagerly took several puffs. A dark possibility had now crept into his mind, filling his head with horror. 'These murders . . . according to some of your notes and what you've told me, it would appear that . . . well, that the bodies have disappeared.'

'That's . . . correct.'

'Just like the graffiti?'

'Just like the graffiti.'

'Hmm . . . ' Smith's mouth puckered. He took another drag from his cigarette and blew smoke from his nostrils. 'So what you're asking me to do is to come up to this godforsaken place to look for invisible dead bodies in the hope that I can see them? That's right, isn't it?'

Thorn hesitated for a moment, his eyes fixed on their destination. His companion had reached the whole point of their trip out here much quicker than he had anticipated, for that indeed was the hope — that Smith would be able to detect, if not *see*, the corpses of the murder victims. 'Yes. That's the hope.'

Smith swallowed a lump in his throat. A cold clamminess came over his skin, raising gooseflesh to his arms. 'Damn you, Thorn! Don't you think I'm in a bad enough state because of you? Now you're dragging me off to some godforsaken village to look for dead bodies.' Regardless of how much he was baulking at the very notion, he was still walking, almost as though he was being drawn, step by reluctant step, towards Heysham Head. 'I can't stand the sight of blood.'

'You'll cope,' replied Thorn, rather unsympathetically.

The familiar wave of despair crashed against Smith's crumbling thoughts. Looking out across the bay and tracing the distant Cumbrian coastline from Barrow-in-Furness as it swooped right past Ulverston towards Grange-over-Sands, Carnforth and Hest Bank, he was struck once again with the dismal reality of his life. Just over three years ago he had been a highly respected professor at one of the world's leading academic institutions. Now he was a shambling ruin of a man, forced to wear handouts, his life largely dependent on alcohol. Stubbornly, he fought the bitterness, channelling it into keeping an equal pace. Just as there was a part of him that wanted to smash Thorn over the head with something sharp and heavy, there was a part of him that wanted to see this through, to pique his dormant fascination. There *was* something very unusual going on here. Perhaps of greater importance, however, was the awareness that he might be able to get something out of this whole experience.

On their left the houses and other assorted buildings thinned out, replaced by the green slopes of an area known as Sandylands. A low wall broken in places by a row of irregular shaped rocks ran parallel to the rusty promenade fence.

Below on the beach, several palisade-like groynes ran out for a short distance from the sea wall.

Smith stopped mid-stride and looked up at one of the houses at the top of the rise. His eyes narrowed. For the briefest of moments he had felt something —

a ripple of unease. Then it was gone.

Up ahead, several large seagulls squabbled over a discarded bag of cold chips. They took to the wing as Smith and Thorn neared, the bag torn and shredded, its contents strewn all over the ground.

'Not many people around, are there?' commented Thorn.

'So?' Smith was glad for small mercies. Just as he hated Morecambrians, he was sure that they despised him. It never occurred to him that he was now unrecognisable — his 'Pervy' Stan persona and appearance having been eradicated by bath water, shaving foam and clean, smart clothes. Nevertheless, all of that could not remove the need for alcohol, and right now his nerves were shrieking for a drink. Thorn had mentioned buying him a meal in a pub called The Royal Hotel. He had to hope that he would not draw attention to himself. A stiffness in his left leg was now making walking difficult. Doggedly, he tried to brush the discomfort to one side, keen now to at least reach Heysham Head. That adventurous impulse which had motivated him through his early academic years — the desire to explore new places and experience foreign cultures — leant him strength that he had long consigned to the waste bin, like so much of his life. Squinting, he could see three lads on BMX-type bikes coming towards them. Instinctively, he prepared to go on the defensive, ready to shield himself from their assault; but in a blur they sped past, clearly uninterested.

'Not far now,' said Thorn.

The stretch of promenade they were on passed a neglected area of open field which had, from a faded sign on a ruined cabin nearby, once been a small putting green. It was now partly overgrown. Further up, there was a playground: a few vandalised swings, a climbing frame and a slide — all of which looked like they had seen better days.

Heysham Village was now becoming

much more distinct.

Individual houses could be seen, the old tiled roofs and smoking chimneys giving the village quite a quaint and timeless attraction. A length of dry stone wall ran along one part of the cliff top, beyond which could be seen a church-yard, headstones and crosses discernible against the deep greens and russet browns. Due to the slope of the land, the uppermost tip of the power station was now shielded from view, enhancing the village's almost storybook charm. Beyond the rooftops could be seen the top fringe of a small wood. Many of the trees were largely leafless, and stood like foreboding and strangely eerie sentinels — natural gravemarkers as opposed to artificial ones. Perched high atop a natural outcropping stood the ruins where they were going.

It was an ideal setting for a murder mystery, thought Smith. In the bright light of early morning it looked very picturesque, but just what it would look like during the hours of darkness he dared not think.

A path to their left sloped up, the promenade now becoming more of a walkway along the top of the sea defences, which sloped down to the beach on their right. Not far up ahead, there stood a squat, stone-built pump house or some such construction. From inside came the faint, constant rumbling of machinery. Just beyond it, a small flight of worn and narrow stone steps led up to the streets of the village proper.

Thorn looked at his watch. It was almost twenty minutes to ten.

'I could do with a drink,' Smith moaned. 'I've got a throat like sandpaper . . . and my legs are killing me.' He was just about to add something else to his list of ailments, anything just to make Thorn feel guilty, when he saw a figure in dark, tattered rags coming towards them, a tall wooden cross with a board and parts of a skeleton nailed to it, held aloft. Atop one of the crosspieces perched a large black bird. Pushing the glasses back on his head, Smith's initial thought was that it was some kind of anti-war protestor all dressed up to look like a mutilated casualty, its condemned effigy raised high. He had seen such demonstrators whilst at Oxford; usually students or anarchists ranting against vivisection practices or the unethical awarding of honorary doctorates to controversial heads of state and other 'unworthies'. This was something else, however.

Thorn tensed, aware that something had Smith spooked.

Now that the individual was less than a hundred yards distant and approaching fast, Smith could see that it was, or at least looked like, a man. His dishevelled features, although largely hidden by the long loop of cowl and hood that covered his head, were diseased-looking — unsightly boils and a rash covering much of one cheek, his chin and throat. A stained eye-patch covered one eye. He was gaunt; his limbs, like his neck and torso, slightly elongated, as though he had been wracked to near breaking point. With the towering skeleton, the whole thing must have been about seventeen feet high. The hand that clutched the wooden cross-mounted pole was wrapped with filthy bandages. The figure looked like something out of a medieval leper colony or the London Dungeon.

Smith froze and brought his hands to his face in sheer terror.

The rag man kept walking, each long stride bringing him closer.

Now less than thirty yards away, Smith could see that what he assumed was a cross was in fact a ghastly crucifix. The skeleton — the Christ image — had been pulled open, bone and glistening red innards displayed for all to see. The head, with its little crown of thorns, was little more than a pecked-clean skull. He felt a scream surging up from his lungs and into his throat, even as the crow dived into the exposed ribcage and shook loose a mess of carrion.

With a bloodcurdling caw from the crow, the rag man strode past. Oblivious to Thorn's cries, Smith stared at the departing apparition — certain that was what he had seen. It was horrible to behold — the way the thing continued to stride, brazenly unafraid to be walking in the bright morning sunlight. Such graveyard wraiths, from all he had read and studied, should be confined to the darkest, most unhallowed deeps. A message, scrawled in lettering that was now only too familiar, on the spectre's placard, below the contorted skeleton, heralded the apocalyptic pronouncement he had seen before:

PREPARE
FOR HE IS COMING

Smith feared that at any moment the thing would turn and reappear directly before him and that he would find himself gazing into a pair of soulless, dead eyes.

'Get a grip of yourself, man!' cried Thorn. 'Tell me what you've seen. Was it another of your nightmares?'

Unsteadily, Smith lurched to one side, certain that he was going to vomit. After a few dry retches, he regained some level of composure and began to take some long deep breaths, strings of spittle hanging from his mouth. With some level of disbelief, he could still see the diseased entity, its form now small and perhaps a tenth of a mile distant as it made its way towards Morecambe. His eyes widened in shock to see the kids on their bikes returning and heading straight for it. Then they were past, no obvious visible interaction taking place between the two parties.

'Tell me what you saw. I need to know.'

Smith shuddered. His cheeks swelled and with a sideways lurch, he did throw up this time, undigested breakfast croissant and bacon splattering on the ground in roughly the same spot Christ's entrails had landed — although thankfully they had now gone. A deep, throbbing migraine was now compounding his troubles.

'What was it? What did you see?'

'What do you think I saw, Thorn? The cast of the Moscow State Circus?' Smith reached yet again for an imaginary bottle. On finding nothing, he took some more deep breaths before continuing. 'It was a ghost . . . a leprous ghost of a man. It looked like he had the Black Death. He carried a banner, which had that message on it. It also had a corrupted crucifix, with an eviscerated Christ figure on it. And there was a bird. A crow or possibly a raven. It was eating Christ's insides. Pecking away at the guts!'

Thorn looked back along the way they had come. 'And . . . has it gone?' There was neither fear nor alarm in his voice.

'I can still see it, if that's what you mean. It's away over there, near that playground. It's heading the way we've come.'

'Let's get up to the ruins before anything else happens. It could be that although you could see it, it couldn't see you, or me for that matter. If that's the case then obviously we should be able to use that to our advantage.'

'Wait a minute, will you?' Smith cursed. He held his shaking hands out. 'It's all right for you to say that you didn't see it, but *I* did. Do you think I can just walk around this damned village, nonchalantly turning a blind eye to each passing corpse that I see? Just what the hell is going on here?'

'To answer your first question, I'm rather hoping that you don't turn a 'blind eye' to any paranormal activity that you notice. I'd rather you informed me. As to your second question, I guess that's what we're here to find out.'

Climbing the steps, they soon came to one of the few narrow streets that led through the village. From here they turned right, and in less than five minutes they were within sight of The Royal Hotel.

Smith was really feeling it now. He was tired, confused, and more than a little scared. Thorn, by direct contrast, seemed completely unfazed, his cool self-assured style irking the ex-professor more than a little.

'That's St. Peter's,' said Thorn, nodding towards the stone-grey church that they were now passing on their right. 'We'll have a look in there later.'

The track up to the ruins of St. Patrick's was cobbled and leaf-covered. On their left ran a ten-foot-high stone wall, the cemetery grounds within spitting distance on their right. Gnarled trees loomed within, their branches drooping low and mournful.

Smith looked at the grim ruins becoming visible before him, his eyes taking in the collapsed stone walls, the broken arch, the numerous leaning trees. The slopes around the ruins were of deep-toned greys, with growths of hawthorn, rocks and jutting headstones forming the darkest patches. He glimpsed the ancient statuary in the cemetery nearby, the tortured shapes resembling surrealistic figures, misshapen heads and limbs twisted towards the church like a frozen tableau of anguished souls.

A gust of biting wind struck them both as they reached the top of a few uneven steps, the wide panorama of Morecambe Bay lying before them.

A few yards away were several shallow rock-cut graves and, just like Alf Turner two days before, Smith froze in terror as he saw that one of them contained something that at least resembled a body. There were others.

5

Sunday, December 12th, 2004

'Trevor Whitcomb. Thirty-nine. Child-killer.' Thorn stared at his large, open photograph album — a weighty folder which had been delivered by express courier service along with several other as-yet unopened packages late the previous evening. Inside were over five thousand snapshots of the nation's worst offenders. A rogues' gallery of rapists, murderers, burglars and terrorists stared grimly, defiantly and wickedly back at him. The face of Whitcomb himself was particularly malign, from his lean, wolfish face and his long, straggly hair to the icy stare. A small **666** tattoo close to the hairline on his forehead completed his far-from-choirboy looks.

Smith was seated across from Thorn, his face drawn and tired-looking. Dark circles under his eyes were a visible sign that his night had been troubled, tormented by the frequent warbling of police sirens and the sights he had seen yesterday: three 'bodies', if that was what they could be called, packed snugly into three small, rock-cut graves. He had noticed the first as soon as they had got up onto the flat cliff top, thinking initially that it was nothing more than a dead animal. And yet, as they had neared, he had discredited that notion, certain that what he was looking at was none other than the contorted, almost jellied remains of another human being.

To Thorn, it was just a shallow, empty indentation; and so at his insistence, and fighting back the urge to vomit again, Smith had been given a tape measure and asked to examine the corpse, relating his findings to his companion. To him, and to him alone, the body was tangible — the wet, putty-like flesh cold and pliant, not rigid as he had been expecting. Although he had been able to handle it, able to pull parts from the indentation in which it lay, the flesh always sprang back, rendering attempts to remove it from its context impossible. As spectral autopsies went it had been crude and messy, unprofessional and nauseating, but several interesting facts had been ascertained. The dimensions of the grave in which Trevor's grisly remains lay measured twelve-and-a-half by sixty by seven-and-a-half inches, with a smaller, separate, eight by seven by six-inch indentation at the top.

By the time Smith had checked all the graves, it was clear to him that the 'bodies' were naked, showing no external markings indicative of excessive violence, and yet . . . all had been completely filleted. Two had been found a short distance from the row of graves, closer to the ruined chapel — packed, if anything, even more densely into smaller stone hollows. One was definitely female. On hands and knees he had searched for vital signs of identification, finding Trevor's tattoo but nothing of note on the others. It had been ghastly work.

'Did you hear what I said?' asked Thorn, looking up from his album.

'Trevor Whitcomb. Thirty-nine. Child-killer.' Stifling a yawn, Smith glanced at his watch, noting that it had just gone six in the morning. After discovering the bodies, the rest of yesterday seemed to have gone past in a kind of surreal blur of strange places and stranger faces. He was vaguely aware of having visited St. Peter's Church and having a substantial amount of whisky with lunch or possibly for lunch. It had been mid-afternoon by the time they had got the bus back to the Midland Hotel.

'There may be a pattern developing here, but as yet I'm not sure about the motive.' Thorn lit a cigarette. 'Now that we've managed to ascertain that Whitcomb was one of the victims, it's possible that . . . '

'It's a rite of desecration . . . a corruption . . . a de-sanctifying,' Smith interrupted. He removed his glasses and gave them a wipe. 'Look at the facts. Three graves. Three . . . victims, one of whom — and perhaps the others — was a murderer. From some of that literature you've got on the history of the ruins it would appear that those graves were, in all likelihood, ossuaries — sacred bone repositories. At one time they would have been covered; in fact, I noticed the grave lids for those smaller two nearby, with a carved cruciform symbol on top. However, it would appear that someone, some *thing* — '

'Or organisation?' Thorn interrupted.

'Or organisation,' agreed Smith with a nod, 'is now using them for the deposition of flesh and flesh alone.'

'Why do you think that is?'

'Well, it's widely believed by many cultures and religions that flesh, unlike bone, is intrinsically corrupt or impure.'

'Sins of the flesh,' Thorn mused.

'That kind of thing.' Smith reached for his cup of tepid tea and took a drink. 'So it would appear that *someone* is seeking to desecrate the graves by interring deboned corpses. For what purpose, I don't know; and as to how they manage to do it and then make the bodies invisible and intangible to — '

'Those unable to see the traces of the dead?'

'Well, yes. And this, of course, is the paranormal aspect of this entire mystery.'

'And the relation to the graffiti and that ghost you saw yesterday?'

'Christ knows.'

'Does He?' Thorn closed his photo album, glad not to have to look at its contents for the time being. Whenever he had to consult the photographic collection he was always reminded of a line from Nietzsche: '*And if you gaze for long into an abyss, the abyss gazes also into you.*'

'There are five more graves,' Thorn continued. 'So I take it our killer seeks another five victims . . . in order to complete whatever it is he or she has in mind?'

Smith nodded. 'I'd say that's a distinct possibility.'

'Hmm. Why, I wonder? Just what's the motive?

'I'd guess it's someone with a deep-rooted dislike of the church. A worshipper of the old Celtic gods, perhaps?'

Thorn stubbed out his cigarette. He stood up and paced over to the window, pulled back the flap of bin-liner that covered it and gazed outside. It was very dark and slightly foggy, the street lights along the promenade casting glowing circles of amber-coloured light which formed small, will-o'-the-wisp-like halos of illumination.

'So, what are we up to today?'

Thorn turned around. 'I think we should go to church.'

★   ★   ★

It had been some time since Smith had last been in a car. He felt a little uncomfortable in the leather-bound passenger seat as they sped along the main Heysham Road, sweeping past The Battery and then venturing into Heysham proper. Thorn never bothered with red traffic lights, zooming through them as though they were not there, his speedometer veering towards fifty miles per hour in the thirty miles per hour zone.

'Steady on, Thorn,' cautioned Smith, nervously gripping the seat.

Thorn ignored him, edging the car's speed up towards fifty-five miles per hour.

Like the day before, it was bright and

reasonably sunny, the digital clock on the dashboard now reading 09:36; and Smith was growing increasingly concerned about Thorn's driving. He closed his eyes and muttered a silent prayer to a god he no longer believed in as a double-decker bus up ahead started to pull out in front of them; but, as calmly as anything, Thorn overtook before gliding back over to the left.

'Jesus Christ, man! Are you trying to get us killed?'

'Maybe. But not today,' Thorn replied laconically.

Soon they were passing the Strawberry Gardens pub, where they then took a right onto Knowlys Road, heading towards Heysham Village. The view from along this stretch of road was breathtaking, the bay spread out before them, gilded in a golden glow from the morning sunlight. The tide was far out, barely visible as a glinting sparkle halfway towards the Cumbrian shoreline.

Smith tensed, suddenly reminded of the dishevelled apparition with the crow and the crucifix. With a sudden dark flash of memory the leper's face and its blasphemous placard violated his mind.

'Look!' said Thorn, bringing the car to a stop.

There was a detectable note of unease in Thorn's voice, a slight quavering which sent a further ripple of fear through the ex-professor. 'What?' Smith turned his head, eyes widening in disbelief as he looked to where Thorn pointed.

Less than thirty yards away on the other side of the road, stood upright on a twenty-five foot high lamp post, was a diminutive *thing*. It was no larger than a five-or six-year-old child; and yet it was much more frail-looking, lacking the frame or the body mass. It was wrapped completely in what looked to be white masking tape.

'Thorn?' Smith swallowed a lump in his throat. The size of it reminded him of a photograph a colleague had once shown him of a withered Amazonian pygmy elder. His mind had to be playing tricks . . . and yet, Thorn could see it too. He began to wonder whether it could be a living thing, a freak or an abnormality. A radiation-spawned mutant. It was hideous, yes. Frightening, definitely. 'What in hell's name . . . ?'

The child-mummy leapt down to the pavement. Its movements were juddery, almost as though it were a marionette under the control of a mad puppeteer.

Flicking open the glove compartment, Thorn reached in and drew out an automatic handgun.

With jerky steps, the horror staggered towards them. It was halfway across the road when a yellow transit van smashed straight into it, knocking it flying. A moustachioed man with curly hair gave a casual look out of his open window, thinking perhaps he had run over a hedgehog or a pothole. Like a rag doll tossed by an enraged bull, the wrapped child-thing spun several times in the air, its arms outstretched. It bounced off the road, its head rolling away like a football from its body to rest at the kerb.

Thorn sped off.

Less than five minutes later they pulled up in the small car park opposite St. Peter's Church.

Smith got out. 'Christ, Thorn. You never told me you had a gun.'

'I must have forgotten.' Thorn slammed his door shut. Hands in pockets, he stalked towards the church.

'What . . . what do you think that thing back there was?'

Thorn looked over his shoulder. 'How the hell should I know?'

It was an honest enough response, for Smith himself had no explanation. He waited a moment in order to try and steady his nerves. The thing had been truly ghastly. Taking a deep breath, he shrugged his shoulders and strode over to where Thorn stood waiting at the entrance to the old churchyard. 'So what's your plan? Why have we come back here?'

'Yesterday, when we had a look around, I noticed something which, I think, warrants further investigation.'

Smith could not remember much of yesterday, the deflated corpses up at the ruins nearby being the only solid memory. He glanced at his watch, noting that it was now ten minutes to ten.

A few parishioners started to shamble

up the path from the village main street, heading for the church. There was nothing particularly noteworthy about them. One old boy hobbled along at the back on two walking sticks. He looked more dead than alive.

Thorn tried to smile, to at least adopt the veneer of friendliness as the villagers filed past him.

'What are you hoping to find out?' Smith asked. From inside the church he could hear faint organ music.

'I just want to take another look at that stone.'

'Which stone?'

Thorn grinned. 'The hog-backed stone.'

A snippet of memory came back to Smith and he was half-aware of standing over a lump of curved grey stone.

Thorn's eyes narrowed as he studied the churchyard, tracing the stone path that led from the outer gate where they were stood, up to the church door. 'What's that?' He started forward, coming to an abrupt halt after less than twenty paces, Smith close behind him.

Surprisingly, both had missed it on

their first visit. It was a trough-shaped piece of stone filled with rainwater.

'It's one of those stone graves,' commented Smith. 'What's it doing here?'

'Don't know. I'll have to see about getting some more historical information together. See if I can't track down an archaeological report or two. Anything that might shed further light on this churchyard and the one up on the cliff.' Thorn reached into a pocket for his cigarette packet. 'This whole area is an English Heritage site.' He lit up. 'We might as well take this opportunity to have a brief look around the cemetery. We'll wait until the service is over before going inside. When we visited yesterday I was pretty sure that I stood on a trapdoor in the aisle leading up to the pulpit. It would be interesting to find out what's down there.'

'Probably just old church records and — '

'Exactly. Some of them might be worth inspecting.'

'Why not just ask the vicar or rector or whatever he is? I'm pretty sure you could get him to let us have a look.'

Thorn nodded. Leading the way, he turned around the edge of the church and headed along one of the paths in the graveyard. From a cursory glance, he could see that many of the headstones dated to the early 1900s, with one or two that were noticeably older. Fresh flowers had been lain in little funeral pots near some of the graves, but most were bare and desolate.

The portion of cemetery they were now entering sloped downhill slightly, ending at a head-high stone wall, beyond which was the cliff which reached down to the rock-strewn shore.

The organ music had now ended.

'Have you noticed how there seems to be a high occurrence of the name 'Hannah'?' Thorn asked, discarding his cigarette. He pointed to a crumbling headstone, the lettering weathered and barely readable. 'Matthew Hannah, 1841-1873. Over there, John Hannah, 1819-1851.'

'There are more over here,' said Smith. 'William Hannah, 1799-1831.' He knelt down to examine another, rubbing away the moss which covered much of the cold stone. 'Jeremiah Hannah. There's a date: March 13th, 1879.'

Thorn looked over to his left where the graveyard ended, the hawthorn-covered railing giving way to the large irregular-shaped boulders, atop which the older remains of St. Patrick's Chapel stood. Near there, seemingly located within its own designated rectangular boundary of spiked fence, was what looked like a squat stone coffin. 'What's that?' he asked, striding determinedly towards it. Upon nearing it, he could see that it was indeed contained within its own boundary of spiked fence, its carved stonework crumbling and weathered. Several large cracks zigzagged their way across the lid, but none were deep enough to permit a view of the coffin's contents. The drooping branches of a lone yew tree seemed to lean down towards it, caressing it like a grieving banshee.

'It's delineated; set within its own boundary.'

'What's the relevance?'

'Well, I seem to remember reading

something about how those unworthy of interment within hallowed ground were buried outside it. Non-Christians. Practitioners of witchcraft. Suicides. That kind of thing.' Grasping part of the railing, Smith peered closer, trying to make out any of the inscriptions on the coffin's flanks. Nothing was readable. A sudden flash of white between the trees and hedgerows over towards the entrance to the churchyard caught his eyes and set his heart thumping.

It was the small, wrapped, headless mummy-thing.

Noticing his companion's open-mouthed stare, Thorn turned around.

Both men stood watching as the taped-up headless monstrosity hesitated at the cemetery gate, almost as though it were mustering the will to enter the consecrated grounds. It clearly gained the power from somewhere, for it stumbled forward onto the path — its movements wooden, like before, yet animated as though it were being tugged along or suspended on invisible wires. It danced crazily, both arms and one leg bent back at unhealthy angles due to its previous impact with the yellow van.

Grabbing the older man by the arm, Thorn made a run for the church. It was only fifty or so yards, but the fear of the thing getting there before them and blocking their way — or else tripping over a headstone and flying headlong towards it — filled that short distance with terror. Reaching the stout wooden door, Thorn unceremoniously kicked it wide and dragged Smith inside, slamming the door behind him.

Several surprised parishioners seated at the back of the church threw them black looks, clearly unaccustomed to such a brash and disruptive entrance. From his pulpit, the rector gave them a similarly disparaging gaze before continuing with his sermon.

'What do we do?' Smith hissed. Due to the acoustics within the old vaulted building, his words echoed much louder than he had intended, drawing a second round of disgruntled looks and mutters.

'Shhhh!' a bald-headed man hissed.

'Thorn, you got me into this — ' started Smith.

'Will you please be quiet?' cried the rector.

Unconcerned with what the rector had just said, Thorn glanced around for anything of use. He had left his gun in the car and what he needed right now was an appropriate weapon just in case it came to that. Leaning against a nearby wall, he saw an old-fashioned window-pole. Rushing over, he snatched it up.

'*Excuse me*,' the rector started as several others in the small congregation turned around, clearly confused and wondering just what all the fuss was about. 'May I enquire as to — ?'

With a crash, one of the small arched stained-glass windows over to Smith's left exploded as the mummy-horror sprang inside. Landing awkwardly on an empty wooden pew, fragments of coloured glass all around it, it righted itself before hopping to the floor. Scuttling like a hideous beetle, it scampered under a neighbouring pew before emerging onto the main aisle.

An old woman screamed and backed away, her face cut from flying glass.

Another elderly lady stared at the

wrecked window and crossed herself, obviously believing that the church was under assault from Beelzebub Himself.

And yet, despite the panic, it was clear to Thorn that the churchgoers were still blind to the tape-bandaged thing. He watched, knuckles whitening around the wooden window-pole, as two men tried to assist the wounded woman and restore calm to those clearly frightened, the thing crawling unchallenged in their midst.

If the parishioners could not see it, however, the rector could. 'In God's name!' With a cry of outrage and horror, he bounded from his pulpit, his Bible raised in the hope that it and the word of God would cast out the evil.

Now that the abomination was inside, Smith turned his self-preservational thoughts to getting out. He ran as fast as he could for the door, horrified to find that it had been locked from the outside. Frantic, he tugged at the door handle, his heart thumping in his chest. Somehow he knew that the puppet-thing was after *him* and *him* alone.

Thorn stepped in to confront it,

jabbing several quick spear-like thrusts. The hook-like tip on the window-pole was old and rusty; and to his shock it fell away after the second strike, clattering to the floor.

People were screaming in mixed shock and alarm.

With a sudden spring, the little taped-up being leapt at Thorn. Arms extended, it grasped him around the neck; and despite the size and mass difference, it managed to overbear him, knocking him back and forcing him over a wooden pew.

More screams of alarm rang out as people gawped in disbelief. In their eyes, it appeared as though the smartly dressed man had become possessed, or else had gone stark-raving mad — for to them he was battling an invisible opponent.

The surreal craziness was becoming more anarchic, as now the rector was in on the act. 'God grant me strength!' Thundering his holy declarations, he smashed the weighty Bible down onto Thorn's attacker's head. Little orange-red flames and smoke leapt into the air, filling his nostrils with the stench of corrupt soul. He repeated his actions, the brass-clasped tome seemingly wailing with mixed glee and objection. 'Out! Foul demon!' he cried. With a third *thwack*, he sent the thing reeling into the stunned crowd of onlookers.

Nursing his bruised throat, Thorn got to his feet. Grabbing the dropped window pole in both hands, he raised it above his head and then brought it down, snapping it painfully over his right thigh. Armed now with two pieces of pole, he stood his ground.

It sprang for the rector this time. Grabbing him by his clerical vestments, it whirled around him, tightening the purple stole around his throat before maliciously hauling him towards the nave and the altar. Thorn beat at it, yet still it pulled the unfortunate man along, his face turning red as the scarf garrotted him. With fiendish delight, the taped-up headless imp somehow manhandled him, cracking his face on the base of the marble inlaid altar, bursting his nose and lips and knocking the communion goblet flying.

With a cry of rage, Thorn plunged both

sharp-pointed lengths of pole deep into the thing's back. Black coffee-like goo dribbled from the two wounds as, with a further grunt of anger, he lifted the struggling terror off the ground and upended it into the carved stone font. Smoke hissed and boiling holy water spat. As though it had been dumped into a scalding bath, the thing went into a frenzied thrashing, desperate to get clear. Despite Thorn's attempts to pin it down, it managed to escape, some of its adhesive covering now burnt and peeling, revealing blackened blister-popped flesh beneath.

One concerned parishioner hobbled to the rector's aid. The majority of the others were clamouring at the door — eager, along with Smith, to get out.

With a series of strikes, Thorn beat the shrunken mummy-thing into a corner. It was damaged, there was no doubt about that, but it seemed incapable of dying — if indeed it lived. Wrapped and steaming, as though it had just emerged from a super-heated sauna, it shook and vibrated, its movements completely unnatural. Darting and ducking beneath Thorn's swings, it hopped bizarrely down the central aisle, weaving a maniacal path straight for Smith.

Eyes widening in terror, the ex-professor raised his hands as it closed in . . .

6

Monday, December 13th, 2004

Morecambe had more than its share of single mothers, many of them unfortunate victims of domestic abuse and circumstance, unable to get any foothold on the proverbial rungs of the social ladder. While some tried to do their best to support themselves and their families, others fell by the wayside, becoming prostitutes or junkies. Others, like 'Troll', became benefit-scrounging misfits, down-and-out shamblers whose only purpose in life seemed governed by the Old Testament teaching of 'Go forth and multiply'. At present tally she had eleven children, including two sets of twins and one lot of triplets.

Like so many in Morecambe, her existence was one that lacked any history, for no one knew anything about her background. The identity of the father or fathers of her many children remained equally mysterious, for she was never seen with any man — a fact that led many to believe that she was not the sole maternal progenitor of her sizeable brood. Nonetheless, like a mother duck, no matter where she went, there was sure to be at least five or six of her offspring in tow.

Small and dumpy, she looked like a cross between an aged Red Indian squaw and something unpleasant from Tolkien's *The Lord of the Rings.* Her forehead sloped brutishly and her face was constantly wrinkled into a sullen, grumpy frown. Her lower lip jutted out well beyond her flattened nose. No matter the weather — rain or shine — she was always dressed in the same old black raincoat. Wherever she went, along came her shopping trolley and small army of porters.

Having now done her morning shopping, 'Troll' left the Morecambe Morrisons store and was making her way to the front, six kids laden with plastic carrier bags shuffling behind her, when the heavens opened and the rain started to pelt down.

At double speed the children shuffled on, a chain of human suffering, shackled together like slaves by the bonds of a violently imposed matriarchy.

By the time they reached the bus stop they were all soaked and shivering. They packed in, tightly huddling under the plastic roofing of the small shelter as the rain continued to lash down. It was dark as well, almost like night, the distant hills over in the Lake District barely visible as darker smudges on the horizon.

It was a horizon 'Troll' had stared at on thousands of occasions, her life spent almost perpetually walking to and fro along this mile or two of seafront. As far back as she could remember, this was all there had been — a daily trudge from where she lived in an overcrowded, barely furnished squat in Heysham, into Morecambe to get her shopping.

Glumly, they all just stood and waited for the rain to cease. Looking out across the bay, she could see that the tide was now almost in, white-flecked waves rolling inland.

Ten minutes passed.

A large double-decker bus pulled up, debouching several sad-looking passengers, prompting 'Troll' to herd her children away in order for them to get past. She shook her head, silently letting the bus driver know that she had no desire to get on board. She heard the engine start up and then the doors closed.

The bus pulled away.

A gigantic octopoid head peered from over the rim of the horizon — a prodigious mountain-sized bulk that towered over the raging sea.

'Troll' reeled back. Before her mind cracked into a million distraught pieces, she was sure that she saw a massive scaled hand resting atop the distant mountains, just as she was certain that the tentacled face transformed into that of her long-dead father.

* * *

Bill Dapper owned a small newsagent's along one of the numerous side streets which ran through Morecambe's West

End. He was a cantankerous old sod who had little time for anyone bar himself. This dark and dreary lunchtime he stood at his counter leafing through the pages of last week's *The Visitor*. For some morbid reason, he particularly enjoyed perusing the large obituaries section, always on the lookout to see if any one he knew had passed away. For, aside from his duties in the shop, he was also a frequent funeral-goer; a dedicated pseudo-mourner; a ghoul who tacked himself onto the funerals of those he knew and those he did not — largely in the hope that he would get some free food out of it. A sponger of 'cold meats' funeral buffets, some went as far as to say he even smelled of the grave.

The shop was old and musty, a throw-back almost to the early 1970s. Certainly, much of his merchandise harkened back to that decade — the candy bars, the crisps and the fizzy drinks more collector's items than edible treats for the sweet-toothed. His joke toys were similarly out-of-date with the present generation of mischief-makers. 'Might as well just give the kids o' today machine guns an' grenades an' be done wi' it,' was one of his popular remarks whenever an adult inquired about children's party paraphernalia — which was not often. Gone were the days of whoopee cushions, stink bombs and electric handshake buzzers.

His eyes widened upon noticing that Gertrude Wakefield had died. She had been his old next-door neighbour before moving to somewhere in Bare after the demise of her husband. Apparently she had been murdered, her body having been found washed ashore on the beach near Bolton-le-Sands, not three miles away.

He was already salivating at the prospect of another 'wake-feast'.

So far this morning he had had only three customers.

He was of half a mind to close early and just go back upstairs to bed, when he heard sounds of someone or something rummaging about in his back room. Alarmed, he edged towards the door at the back of the shop, eyes darting from side to side, searching for the cricket bat he kept in readiness to deter thieves. The shop had been broken into numerous times despite the wire-meshed shutters and the triple security bolted doors. This time he was determined to take the law into his own hands. It would not be the first time he had resorted to such violence. Five years ago he had run over a fleeing teenager after chasing him from his shop. Still alive after the initial collision, he had reversed over him once or twice to finish the job.

Somehow he had escaped a custodial sentence, the prosecuting judge accepting his barrister's appeal for understanding on the grounds that he was mentally impaired and that he had acted in perceived self-defence.

Again came the sounds of someone moving about in his storeroom. It was a heavy, watery sound, as though a soaked mop was being slapped on the floor.

Grabbing hold of his cricket bat, he gingerly reached for the door handle, an overpowering fishy stink assaulting his nostrils. He threw it open, his admittedly deranged mind shattering at what he saw.

And, in an ironic twist of fate, he would become a 'cold meat' offering.

★ ★ ★

Patricia McGuiness suffered from a severe form of delusional paranoia, though on the day of her actual 'brain-melt' what she witnessed was, in a perverse way, reality. Since childhood — and more particularly after the recent Halloween — she had been experiencing weird sensations and succumbing to lengthy phases of what had to be some form of psychological dementia. Hardly a single hour — whether awake, or sleeping — had gone by when she had not felt that she was being threatened by something. In her waking hours, common items as seemingly harmless, innocuous and in-offensive as a spoon or a toilet roll would become possessed with a malign energy; ready, and willing, to leap down her throat or spring at her and blind her. To her, an open tin of spaghetti would became a monstrous foe; the cold noodles slithered like dead brain matter from the pan into which thet had been poured, the protoplasmic bubbles amorphous and slimy. 'O Jaysus! *Jaysus!*' she would cry,

138

battling to keep the aggressive pasta at bay with a wooden spoon.

Hung-up coats were another source of fear — for in her deranged mind they were animate beings poised to lash out at her from where they dangled, to flail her with their arms and suffocate her with their weight. Additionally, she dreaded the phone ringing, for it was always the same tinny voice screeching down the line: *'The Russians are comin'! The Russians are comin'! They're comin' for you!* Hello, is that Mrs. McGuiness? Can you hear me?'

Screaming, she would slam the receiver down.

From the clock on the kitchen wall — another wicked entity which at times spoke to her — she could see that it was now just after two in the afternoon. She had planned on inviting her neighbour, Netta, round for drinks and a chat, but after the last time she knew that she had better be more prepared. It had been highly embarrassing when the sofa had turned on her neighbour, the soft pillows munching and gnawing like vicious guard dogs. Once 'Nervous' Netta, as she called her, had gone, she had beat the sofa to within an inch of its upholstered life with a shovel she had found in the garage. That would teach it for trying to devour her guest. Staring at the piece of furniture, she wondered whether it was time to get the shovel again.

Like most sofas, it just sat there, obediently minding its own business.

Still . . . maybe it was just waiting . . .

She pointed a finger at it, defying it to do anything untoward, warning it to be on its best behaviour. Next time she would burn it. She kept a can of petrol and a large box of matches in the cupboard under the stairs for just that emergency.

Her unspoken threat over, she considered going to the phone but held back, trying to think what else she had planned for the day. She thought she had two children, a son and a daughter, both as equally out of step with reality as her. Both were currently at school, no doubt learning how to repair ostriches or something, and she had to try and get by without them. Her only real friend — even though she was not — was Netta.

Netta. Netta. *Oh Netta.*

If only Netta was here, she thought. Netta would know what to do, providing the sofa or the coats or the spaghetti in the cupboard didn't get her.

Should she give her a ring? Well, should she?

What if it was Boris Yeltsin on the line . . . *again?* What would she say? *Dear Boris, I would appreciate it if you stopped phoning me at all hours. People will start talking and start thinking that I'm a spy working for the KGB. I'm just a crazy, severely schizophrenic Irishwoman living in a dying Lancashire seaside resort. My time serving in the Spetsnaz special forces was long ago . . .*

There came a loud knock on the front door.

Patricia's heart leapt.

Nervously, she stared all around, checking that none of the furniture — the sofa in particular — was preparing for battle. Cautiously, she edged past the hung-up coats. 'Is that you, Netta?' she whispered, trying to define the silhouette on the other side of the opaque glass window. Netta was short and dumpy. This figure was tall and thin. That was enough to make her even more frightened. 'Netta?' she repeated, warily.

Her visitor rapped the door again.

'Is that you, Netta?' Hands shaking, Pat quickly lit a cigarette. She looked down as the letterbox, set at ankle height, creaked open — the sound strangely amplified, making it sound like a door opening in a haunted house.

Something other than a letter started to slink through the narrow gap. Like rancid jelly, the thing from beyond the door seemed to almost flow through the letterbox before plopping like molten wax onto the carpet. Once part of it was through the door it began to reform, to solidify, coalescing into an amorphous mass, more goo continuing to pulsate in sickly peristaltic motions.

It stank to the high heavens.

Whereas a normal, sane individual would probably have run away screaming, heading for the back door or barricading themselves in the bathroom, the mad Irishwoman just stood there, her long fingers raking through her tangled hair. '*Netta?*' she said as her 'friend' continued to ooze through the letterbox. 'I was goin' to phone you.'

★ ★ ★

Not for the first time in recent days, Smith woke up in a strange bed in an unfamiliar room. His sight was blurry, so leaning to his right he was relieved to find his spectacles resting on a small bedside cabinet. He put them on, his surroundings now swimming into focus. It was undoubtedly a private ward of a hospital he was in, the furnishings all too recognisable for someone who had spent weeks in hospital after being knocked off his bike in central Oxford many years ago. A sudden wave of disorientation hit him, causing his mind to reel in a drunken spasm.

A door opened and Thorn entered.

Smith retched dryly.

'Would you like some water?' Thorn

asked, moving closer. Without waiting for an answer, he filled a small plastic cup from a nearby sink and gave it to Smith.

Smith sat up and took a sip.

'We're in Oxford, just in case you wanted to know. You're in a private wing of the Radcliffe Infirmary. Strictly secret, of course,' Thorn added.

Smith was too out of it to respond. He just took another sip.

'It's Monday.' Thorn looked at his watch. 'Five minutes to six in the evening.' He sat down on a nearby chair.

Blearily, Smith continued to take in his surroundings. The room was small yet pristine, a faint smell of medicine and cleaning agent lingering in the air.

'Don't worry. Physically, there's nothing wrong with you . . . aside from high blood pressure and, well, slightly damaged liver functions.'

'Why am I here?' Smith asked, his words laboured.

'Well.' Thorn pulled his chair a little nearer. 'Maybe you can answer that question.' He was just about to reach for something by the bed when Smith began to convulse, his hands clawing the air before him as though trying to fend off an invisible assailant.

'*The headless child!* It's coming for me!' Smith screamed, his eyes wide in terror. 'The bandaged demon!'

'Snap out of it, man!' Thorn cried, grabbing the ex-professor's arms and pinning them down. 'You killed it. It's no longer a threat.' He was about to say more, but from the glazed look in the older man's eyes it was clear that he had once again slipped into unconsciousness. Probably for the best, he thought. He stood up, moved to the other side of the bed and checked to ensure that the tape recorder was still working before leaving the room.

7

Tuesday, December 14th, 2004

Smith was propped up in bed, just finishing the last of his grapefruit, when Thorn entered carrying a newspaper. He looked up, took a pip from his mouth and placed it in his empty bowl.

'How are you?'

Smith sensed that the question was asked without any real sincerity. To Thorn he was just a necessary ally, a useful means to an end — although what exactly that end would be, he dreaded to think. 'Better. In fact, I feel quite good, if truth be told.'

'Excellent.' Without any other comment, Thorn opened his newspaper and passed it across. 'Thought this might interest you. It's the most recent *Lancaster Gazette*.'

The highlighted headline instantly caught Smith's eye:

RASH OF STRANGE OCCURRENCES IN SEASIDE TOWNS

He read on:

A spate of bizarre happenings have been reported by several reliable eyewitnesses in the vicinity of Morecambe and Heysham. On Saturday, 11th December, several people, including an off-duty special police officer who declined to be named, claimed to have seen what can only be described as ghostly sightings and other unnatural occurrences. As a further matter of interest, eleven people were arrested for minor acts of antisocial behaviour and three others were deemed in need of imminent psychiatric assistance. The authorities have yet to announce whether these events are in any way linked.

'It looks like we're entering the next phase.'

Smith lowered his glasses and looked at Thorn. 'Meaning what?'

'Well, it would now appear that others

are becoming susceptible. Others are now becoming aware of what initially only you could see.'

Smith re-read the short article before handing the paper back.

'As soon as you're properly rested — '

'I'm ready now,' Smith interrupted.

'All right. I'll let you get dressed and then we'd better get down to business. I've discovered quite a bit that might be of interest whilst you've been recuperating. And I'm sure you'll want to know exactly what happened after our little encounter with the paranormal at St. Peter's.' Thorn turned and made his way towards the door. He glanced at his watch. 'I'll return for you once I've had a bit of lunch at the canteen here. Let's say, one o'clock.' He opened the door and left.

Smith was ready with ten minutes to spare by the time Thorn returned.

Inconspicuously, they exited the bustling hospital — no discharge forms to sign, no doctor to consult, none of the normal red tape seeming to apply to them — before getting into a black car and driving south out of the city and into the surrounding countryside. It was clear, it was bright and it was just over two hundred miles from Morecambe, and that in itself did wonders in lifting the ex-professor's spirits.

'Where are we going?' Smith asked as he gazed out of the car's reflective windows.

'Lower Hampton. It's a small village about eight miles from here.'

'One of your . . . safe houses?'

'That kind of thing.' With no further talk, Thorn concentrated on driving.

The journey took less than twenty minutes, allowing Smith a brief amount of time to just sit back, relax and enjoy the journey. They were soon out of the university city, the countryside picturesque and pleasing in the early afternoon sunlight.

Upon entering Lower Hampton, they took a left off the main road and turned down a private drive. Gravel crunched under the tyres as the car came to a stop at a large wooden door set into a high stone wall outfitted with security cameras.

Thorn got out and punched a code into an electronic door lock, and moments later the door began to slowly open. He got back in the car and drove up another long drive to a very expensive-looking property. Ivy climbed up one length of wall and stone gargoyles perched along the crenellated rooftops. There was a stone fountain in the garden as well as several more outbuildings.

Everything reeked of wealth and college property, reminding Smith of the houses in north Oxford where he used to live. When the car came to a stop, he unbuckled his seatbelt and got out, noting that the outer gate had now swung shut. He slammed the door, the noise startling the ravens from their nests high in the nearby trees.

Two Dobermans sat like sentinels on either side of the front door.

With a click, Thorn opened the car boot and withdrew a black briefcase and several folders. Closing the boot, he turned to Smith. 'I think it's best if we get to work straight away. There's a lot we have to go through.' He headed for the house. 'Don't worry about the dogs. This way.' Upon reaching the front door, he patted both guard dogs and punched in another security code before turning the handle. Entering the hallway beyond, he progressed down a poorly lit corridor which smelled of age and neglect before reaching a curtained-off stairwell, Smith trying to keep up behind him.

'Is there no one else here?'

'Just a basic domestic staff,' Thorn answered, flicking a light switch. 'A cook. A gardener. A housekeeper. Nothing extravagant.' He started up the stairs. 'Be careful. The stairs twist and turn and get quite narrow in places.'

Like most old houses, the stairs were indeed tortuous, with several narrow landings leading to small out-of-place doors and hatchways. Some of the treads creaked under Smith's feet and on more than one occasion he had to save himself from a serious tumble with an out-stretched hand. They seemed to go up for at least three floors, and then down one, although it was nigh on impossible to really tell.

'Almost there.'

They came out onto a landing with several very old oak doors.

'Here we are.' Thorn paced forward and opened the door facing them. 'After you.'

From the doorway, Smith could see that the room was small and appeared to be very cluttered with piles of books and papers heaped untidily all over the floor. It was reasonably well lit, daylight coming in through the small leaded windows and —

He stopped, eyes widening in confusion. His mouth dropped open as he stared to his left, noting the shelves crammed with books and rolled maps. Straight in front of him he could see a large wooden desk, on top of which rested an old typewriter, more books, a pending tray, an old-fashioned globe, a pyramid paperweight, and other miscellaneous bits and pieces he thought he recognised. Glancing to his right, he saw a tall wooden coat-stand, several metal filing cabinets, a coffee-making machine and more laden bookshelves.

It was his office, just as he had left it!

A powerful wave of déjà-vu surged through Smith, causing him to rock unsteadily on his feet. Familiarity tempered with disbelief pounded at his brain. He staggered to one side, supporting himself on the door jamb. 'How?' he mumbled.

Thorn smiled. 'Well, it wasn't easy, but I hope it's worth it.'

Crossing the threshold, Smith felt as though he had gone back in time. Everything was, more or less, just as he had left it back in early 2001. 'You forgot the ashtray,' he commented weakly, surveying his desk.

'I believe one of your students stole it,' Thorn replied. 'After you walked out, I salvaged what I could and brought it here. Your books and folders, your documents and field notes. All is just as you left it.' He pointed to two large, sealed cardboard boxes lying close to the coat-stand. 'That is, with the exception of what you'll find in those.'

Smith was only half-listening, still trying to take in this almost perfect snapshot of his past. He was half-expecting it to melt away like a cruel illusion as he paced, almost reverently, over to his old desk. With a tenderness that certainly belied his demeanour of late, he reached out and ran his hand over the polished wood, stroking the dark pine as though it were a coffin in which lay a recently deceased loved one. Slowly raising his head, he scanned the rows of books, the names of familiar titles, authors and colleagues flooding back through time to remind him all the more of the man he had once been. He noticed several of his own detailed works amongst the anthropological library. A lump formed in his throat, his eyes watering.

'We've got work to do,' said Thorn. 'So take a seat.'

Smith looked at his old chair for a moment, lost in his own thoughts.

Thorn had already drawn up a chair and had now opened his briefcase. He looked up. 'Sometime today would be nice.'

Smith sat down, still unable to fully accept the reality of his surroundings. It *was* his study. His office. It even looked to be about the same size. Everything from the carpet to the wallpaper to the layout was nigh on identical. The books were all as he had ordered them. The bits of paperwork scattered haphazardly over the carpet were as he had left them. Without being fully aware of what he was doing, he opened a drawer and was not entirely surprised to find the small half-empty bottle of port and two glasses he kept for special visitors.

'You remember this?' Thorn slid a sheet of paper across the desk. It was a good-quality photocopy of a photograph, the front and back of the strange lump of stone with its myriad carved scenes clearly visible. 'It's the hog-backed stone from St. Peter's. I think it may hold the key.'

Reaching across, Smith picked up the piece of paper.

'According to some of the scant details I've managed to unearth, the two sides of the stone relate to the two sides of Norse legend and existence — good and evil, law and chaos, light and dark.' Thorn pointed to the uppermost image. 'Although the symbolism is hard to decipher, this surface seems to deal with chaos, as high-lighted by the preponderance of wolves and snakes.' He pointed to a prone man-like figure. 'This guy may represent mankind. The approaching wolf — the power of evil or darkness — all set to devour him. On this side . . . '

'I'll stop you there,' Smith interrupted, much to Thorn's surprise. The familiarity of his surroundings had done wonders in restoring some of his old self-confidence. He rose from his chair and went to a bookcase, returning with a well-thumbed leather-bound book. Taking his seat once more, he opened the book, leafing through several pages before coming to the page he sought. An old woodcut-type of illustration showed a large wolf licking at the face of a man tied to a stake. 'This is it. This man here, with the wolf approaching him, is none other than the Norse hero, Sigmund, father of Sigurd, the dragonslayer. According to legend, all of his brothers were offered to the wolf; but his sister, Signy, coated him in honey so that when the wolf came it began to lick it off. Sigmund bit its tongue and killed it. It is this scene which is represented on the hog-back stone.' With an element of smugness, he pointed to the lower image. 'And here, surprise, surprise, is Sigurd himself, stabbing the mighty shape-changing dragon, Fafnir.'

'And the relevance?'

Smith looked up, his eyebrows raised. 'I don't think there is one. I think it's a red herring. Nothing more. The images on this stone are but a mere iconographic testament to Norse legend — Sigmund, Sigurd, Fafnir. Even that rather innocuous-looking tree-like thing. That's Yggdrasil, the so-called 'world tree', which connected the nine planes of the Norse cosmology.' He turned his gaze to the large cardboard boxes. 'What's in those?'

'I'll show you.' Thorn paced over and lifted them one at a time from the floor and placed them on the desk. 'You're going to like this.'

Mildly curious, Smith watched as his associate removed a penknife from a jacket pocket and ran it down the thick tape that sealed the smaller of the two containers.

Thorn hesitated a moment as though to build the tension. 'Prepare to be surprised.' He reached inside, hands delving into the mass of white polystyrene packing foam before lifting free a strange piece of dark curved wood which certainly on first glance reminded Smith of some kind of boomerang. It was only as the mass of yellow, black and red feathers attached to it became visible that he recognised it as an item of elaborate headgear as worn by several of the chieftains of the remoter parts of Papua New Guinea.

'*Christ!*' Smith exclaimed. 'That looks like a . . . '

'A Huli-Wa-wa Wigman's headdress?' Thorn interrupted, his pronunciation uncertain.

'How the hell . . . ?' Smith eyes widened as Thorn pulled out more exotic shamanistic paraphernalia and placed it on the desk before him. 'Where did you come by this?'

'Let's just say that I've 'borrowed' them from the Pitt Rivers Museum. I daresay you're familiar with them?'

'Just a little!'

'Excellent. I thought you would be.' Thorn delved deeper. 'Let's see. What else have we got?' The fingers of his right hand clenched a mass of wiry, long-dead hair and a second later he lifted free a grisly necklace of shrunken heads. He looked at one of them briefly before casually throwing it down on the desk.

There was a time when Smith would have been outraged by the other's cavalier actions, angered at his rather wanton disrespect. Now, however, he couldn't care. So much had happened to him, all of it negative, that he had been channelled into a different state of thinking. He had become tainted by life in Morecambe — had become a completely different person — and for all he knew, such a transformation was irreversible. He remained curious, however, as to how — and more importantly, why — Thorn had bothered to assemble all of these relics. He lifted his gaze from the macabre necklace. 'Would you care to explain?'

'Well.' Thorn paused, gathering his thoughts. 'During your time in hospital you muttered a few words in your sleep. Words which, fortunately, I managed to catch on tape. You muttered about some of these things . . . so, I deemed it necessary to *obtain* them. It turned out to be far easier than anticipated. If you ever regain your position at Oxford you've got to make sure that they tighten up their security. I daresay you're also curious as to why I've gone to such lengths to recreate your office.'

'I *was* wondering.'

'Let's just say that the offer of a permanent place within my organisation has arisen. And . . . well, I've put your name forward. This could be your new base, if you accept.'

'Not bloody likely.' Smith reached for the port.

'Just consider it, that's all I'm asking. Anyway, right now there's something else I'd like you to take a look at. Preferably before you . . . ' He mimed taking a drink and was somewhat relieved to see his associate put the bottle back down.

* * *

Gale-force winds battered the Morecambe and Heysham coastline, driving the sea towards the promenade with a fury not seen in many a year. Smashing into the promenade, huge walls of freezing water pounded the sea defences and rose twenty feet into the air before crashing down and spilling out, flooding many of the low-lying streets and belatedly sand-bagged properties beyond. Idiot drivers tried to negotiate their way through the rivers that only yesterday had been roads, their vehicles sloshing through tyre-deep channels of fast-flowing sea water.

Some talked about climbing aboard what remained of Noah's Ark and weathering out the storm before things escalated to truly Biblical proportions.

Daniel Hoogstratten, however, was not one of them — nor would he ever be. He stood, seemingly transfixed, staring out of the study window of his three-storey Sandylands house as before him Morecambe Bay seethed and thrashed. Distant forks of lightning flashed across Black Combe, the last visible Cumbrian hill on the horizon. Everything outside was dark and gloomy, much as it was inside.

Behind him, sat at a desk not dissimilar

to the one at which Professor Mandrake Smith sat in sunny Oxfordshire, were a man and something else. The man was fat and unsightly; and, had Veronica Crowley been present and not in the Moor Hospital secure unit from which her son had recently been liberated, she would have identified her Barry, despite the discoloured, ravaged skin and deranged look in his now fish-like eyes. The other was weird and hairless. It had a long face like that of the being in Munch's 'The Scream', yet it was both eyeless and noseless, its only facial feature a dark, roughly circular hole for a mouth. It was rocking back and forth and sobbing quietly. Clasped to its chest by long spindly fingers was a grotesque, child-sized head.

All three were bare naked.

'I looked upon the rotting sea. And drew my eyes away. I looked upon the eldritch deck. And there the dead men lay,' muttered Hoogstratten. He cocked his head to one side before turning round, an evil grin on his mad face. It appeared as though he had finally come to a decision regarding their next course of action. The knowledge that someone was actively trying to thwart their plans and had been somewhat successful so far, had come as a minor setback. 'Although the witchling has been taken from us, I believe we can still put him to some use. Give me the head.'

★   ★   ★

The wine cellar was large and spacious, racks of dusty vintages — some covered with cobwebs — forming a maze of narrow passageways which, in the poor light, were proving hard for Smith to navigate. Thorn led the way, coming to an abrupt halt at a large barrel. He twisted the spigot twice anticlockwise, and with a dull grating sound a secret door over to their right swung open. Beyond was a short passage which ended at another door — this one looking far more modern.

'What is this?' Smith asked, bemused.

Without answering, Thorn entered the passage and opened this second door, light immediately spilling out from the area beyond.

The illumination was bright, causing Smith to squint. Tentatively he walked forward, wondering just what new scene he was going to see in this mysterious house.

It was a laboratory of sorts, as evidenced by the numerous computers which chirped and clicked from where they lay on a desk that ran the perimeter of the room. None of which made any sense to Smith. Like many academics of his generation, computers remained an unknown science. Two things did catch his immediate attention, however. The first was the grey-haired woman in a lab coat working in a fume cupboard at the rear of the room, her eyes protected by a set of safety goggles. The second was the sheet-covered operating table in the centre of the room. Something in the lie of the contours of the sheet disturbed him deeply.

The technician obviously saw them, for she stepped from the fume cupboard, slid the protective panel across and removed her goggles. 'Thorn.'

Thorn turned to Smith. 'Let me introduce Doctor Stephanie Harris. A good friend and a damn fine scientist.'

Smith nodded and grunted something inaudible. He was still looking at the operating table, eyes tracing the outline of what lay beneath.

'Any new developments?' Thorn asked.

'Not much, I'm afraid. We've subjected your little friend here to all that we can think of and come up with a few ideas. Like I said, the DNA that we've managed to extract points with a hundred percent certainty to West Indian origin. No doubt about it. Dating the few extant residues has been tricky. Calibrated AMS readings give somewhere in the region of two hundred and twenty to three hundred years old. I can't be any more accurate than that.'

'It would all seem to support my initial theory.'

'The evidence would appear so. Although from our reports it doesn't look as though the grave has been tampered with. Could be that whoever exhumed the body in the

165

first place knew exactly where — '

'Come on, Thorn!' interrupted Smith. 'Is anyone going to tell me what's going on? I've got a pretty bad feeling I know what's under that sheet so let's just get this over with.' Angrily, he stomped forward and pulled back the cover, not entirely surprised to see the dissected remains of his headless adversary from St. Peter's Chapel underneath. Now motionless, it still looked horrible. Worse perhaps. A surgical slice down the midsection had exposed layers of white polystyrene packing and thin wires which no doubt served as a skeleton — there were no longer any true bones present. Its exterior was still wrapped heavily in that white adhesive tape that he remembered only too well. There were no internal organs present to speak of. There was a mild smell of formaldehyde coming from it.

'Ugly, but amazing. Is it not?' commented Thorn.

'What the hell is it?' asked Smith, his face wrinkling in disgust.

'It's hard to say, really. But both myself

and my colleague believe that what you're looking at is the partial remains of a late-eighteenth century West Indian slave boy known as 'Sambo'.'

'*What? Who?*'

'Not far from Morecambe is a place known as Sunderland Point. It's a small coastal community which is regularly isolated by the tide. Historically, the area was used as a base of operation for sea trade with North America and the West Indies. Sugar, cotton, that kind of stuff. Indeed, a pub just a few miles down road, The Golden Balls, is still known locally as 'Snatchems' because it was allegedly used as a tavern where the unsuspecting were press-ganged and thrown onto such trade vessels. Anyway, our dissected friend here would appear to be Sunderland Point's own 'Little Sambo' — a West Indian cabin-boy who, unprepared for northern climes, fell foul of some disease, probably pneumonia. As a non-Christian, he was buried in unconsecrated ground, since when his grave seems to have attracted a certain quasi-shrine-like status.'

'That's all well and good, but . . . ?'

'As to why he's here . . . ' Thorn began. 'Well, I believe that he has been . . . altered.'

'Is that so?' said Smith, sarcastically.

Ignoring the ex-professor, Thorn continued. 'He's also boneless. Just like the corpses we've discovered. Indeed, there's no bone matter to be found whatsoever. Filleted to perfection.' Taking a nearby pair of forceps, he peeled back a layer of sticky coating. 'This is plain, standard, white tape. Plastic. Nothing special. As you can see, the interior of the body had been packed and reinforced with padding and wire, no doubt to prevent it from caving in on itself, and to give it a certain rigidity.'

'But how did it move about? How did it attack me? Where are its batteries?'

'No batteries.'

'What?'

'There are no batteries.' Thorn returned the forceps to the tray. 'Our friend here wasn't some cheap Japanese remote control toy. On the contrary, what we have here is a very complex re-animated being. A homunculus, if that means anything to you.'

Smith knew exactly what Thorn was getting at. 'You mean to say a sorcerer's familiar? A wizard's sidekick?'

'Exactly. 'Sambo' was being used for occult reasons. The worrying thing, certainly from our perspective, is that whoever controlled it is going to be somewhat displeased at our now having it in our possession. According to occult folklore, the separation of such a being from its master is never an easy one. So, it could be that whoever owned 'Sambo' is acutely aware that he has been destroyed.'

'Hang on a minute,' protested Smith. 'This is beginning to get a little too weird for my liking.'

'*Too weird?* You don't recall what happened at St. Peter's, do you? When this devil-doll went for you, you countered with some of your own Papua New Guinean mojo, in effect creating a protective shield of fire, repelling our little friend here.'

Smith's jaw dropped.

'That's right. I told you that you had powers. Latent perhaps, but certainly there. There was more besides the fiery barrier. Once the threat had been kept at bay, you — or whatever guardian entity watches over you — set about going on the offensive. I could see — and I think the rector could as well — smoky, ghost-like shapes beginning to form around you. Like a school of piranha, they latched onto 'Sambo' and began to . . . *eat*, if that's the correct term. The outer casing still bears the bite marks. It was quick. All over in less than maybe twenty seconds. By that time you had collapsed and so I, with the help of the rector, carried you outside. We got you back to my car and, well, the rest is history as they say.'

Smith stood rigid, his mind unable and unwilling to accept Thorn's explanation of events. For the best part of two minutes, he just continued to stare at the headless thing laid out before him. *This could not be real.* None of it. Paranoia crept its unwanted roots into his erudite brain. This was insane — it had to be. So why was Thorn instilling his mind with these crazy notions? Could it be that all he had experienced so far was nothing more than an ingenious and cruel plot to drive him over the edge? Regarding the writing on the walls, the dead bodies and the ghost — he only had Thorn's word that *he* could not see them. They could all just be stage props and actors. The newspaper article could easily have been falsified. He closed his eyes, screwing them shut, hoping that when he opened them again 'Sambo' or whatever-its-name was would be gone. But, despite the fact that he tried to tell himself otherwise, he could see the homunculus in his mind, imprinted on his brain. Headless, it danced and hopped. He opened his eyes to see it was still there. And as to what he had allegedly done to it . . .

'I would have told you sooner, but — ' Thorn started.

'Is that so?' Smith interrupted. He was trying to remain calm and in control; but faced with a situation like this, and having just been told what he had done, it was proving difficult. He swayed on his feet. Supporting himself on the edge of the operating table, he straightened and turned to the woman in the lab coat. 'Are you just another of Thorn's lackeys?'

Doctor Harris smiled. 'Firstly, I'm not

one of Thorn's 'lackeys'. Secondly, parapsychology and science don't normally sit well together. That said, I've seen enough over the years to make me aware that not everything is quantifiable, just as not everything obeys the scientific laws that we think we know. I wasn't present when this thing attacked you; however, I believe what I've been told. The tests I've carried out all seem to indicate that what remains within the artificial exoskeleton of tape was once a human being of West Indian origin. A male of approximately nine or ten, maybe younger. Further tests may substantiate my theory of a Deep One lineage.'

'A what?'

'A possible Deep One lineage.' Doctor Harris looked to Thorn.

'Let's just examine the facts as they stand,' said Thorn, evading the issue. 'This bandaged being attacked us. It entered the church and caused no end of mayhem, attacking the rector before turning on you. Somehow, you conjured your own form of sorcery and managed to destroy it, although in doing so you yourself ended up unconscious for several hours. I think it highly unlikely that the attack was random; therefore we must assume that — '

It sat up.

The three of them pulled back, looks of sheer horror on each of their faces.

Paralysed with terror, Smith felt his throat seize up, air unable to get to his lungs. His eyes widened as the skin on his face tightened. Before him, the headless cut-open remains of 'Sambo' sat bolt upright, its final act of physical movement now complete. The air around the space where the head would be wavered as though a bad projectionist was trying to focus a film on an insubstantial screen. A head, more skull-like in appearance, began to coalesce — although not quite solidify — on the bandaged stump of neck.

Thorn looked about, grabbed a surgical bone saw, and prepared to swing down even as Doctor Harris reached for a camera. But before either of them could act the superimposed head rotated, performed a three-hundred-and-sixty-degree revolution, and vanished.

8

Wednesday, December 15th, 2004

Hoogstratten had been many things in his fifty-four years of life: black magician, Selous Scout, mercenary, treasure hunter and amateur archaeologist. It had been the latter two pursuits that had taken him to Great Zimbabwe, Qustul, Memphis, Ur and a host of other rich archaeological sites. Driven mostly by the desire to discover untold riches and thus earn fame and wealth, he had travelled north through Africa into Europe, believing that was where the wealthier patrons after illicit archaeological finds would be. He had served for a time as an agent, fencing ill-gotten archaeological relics to wealthy buyers, mostly German purchasers of antiquities. Two years ago he had acted as an intermediary between an American colonel operating in Baghdad and a buyer in New York, securing the safe, illegal and clandestine transfer of priceless Sumerian treasures out of Iraq.

His defining moment, however, was his unearthing, or rather rediscovering, of something very strange and powerful in Heysham — in Vicarage Wood to be precise.

A flicker of a smile creased his mouth. He stood, facing out of his Sandylands home's upper window, gazing sternly down onto the empty promenade and out to sea. It was early morning and still very dark. The sky was a sinister black, almost as though what daylight there was, was suffering a hangover from yesterday's storm. It had been fierce, even by Morecambe Bay's capricious standards.

Though he had known worse.

Far worse.

He was mulling things over. The images that his sorcery had granted were blurred. Three figures — one a doctor or a scientist. A laboratory of sorts. Computers. He closed his eyes and began to concentrate, the images he saw in his mind's eye still indistinct — distorted — as though seen through a thick red filter. That one of the trio had power was apparent, for it seemed as though he were shielded to some extent from his probing. He focused harder, concentrating his will on the tall dark-haired man instead. The image of a large run-down hotel appeared in his mind.

★   ★   ★

Smith sat next to Thorn in *The Plough Inn*, Lower Hampton's only public house, the now near-empty whisky glass gripped in his right hand. A sixteenth century former coaching house, it was tastefully decorated throughout, from its three inglenook fireplaces and its raftered beams to its fully modern kitchen and well-stocked bar. Horse brasses featured prominently. Strong memories of his Oxford days when he would frequently partake of a lunctime drink in one of the many choice scholastic drinking establishments flooded back, causing him to be temporarily lost in a flush of nostalgia.

A short, fat, balding man with glasses — not unlike how Smith himself had looked before his self-imposed exile to Lancashire had drained his body of vitality — entered the pub and joined a throng of five others gathered around the bar. For a moment, the likeness was striking, almost causing Smith to drop his glass. Then the moment passed and he finished his drink.

'I'll get another,' said Thorn, rising from his chair.

Smith sat back and watched as Thorn headed for the bar.

It had been Thorn's idea to come out, to try and get some grounding in normality after the ghastly events of yesterday and the week before. It had been a good idea — the pleasant surroundings, the comforting food and the drink had done something to dilute the strangeness that they had witnessed.

Smith marvelled at how unaffected Thorn seemed to be. He watched as his accomplice, whom he knew comparatively little about, ordered a round and chatted to those already there as though he were just a casual professional — a lawyer or a personal finance advisor, judging by his impeccable dress sense; certainly not a paranormal investigator, or whatever his title was. The man remained an enigma. Mind you, was that not the usual description of the stereotypical 'men in black' who policed the supernatural?

Everything — the setting, the people, the feel of optimism and the obvious wealth — contributed to make Morecambe seem a dark dream.

Smith listened casually to the locals' conversations — where they were proposing to educate their children; the state of the local golf club; how their very expensive house renovations were coming on; the preparations for next year's summer fête on the village green, and whether or not it would affect the cricket pitch. This was undeniably middle England, its inhabitants blissfully ignorant of just how grim it was 'up North'.

There was no denying the fact that these were the kind of people Smith had spent almost all of his Oxford life around; and yet the more he heard, the more unbearable the atmosphere in the pub became. What had only a half hour or so before been comforting and reassuring, now filled him with a sense of antipathy. It was unlikely that these people would last longer than a day if they had to live in Morecambe, for these pompous idiots had no idea of what real life was, no concept of hardship or deprivation beyond the infinitesimal problem of who was to run the plant stall at the fête. In many ways they were perhaps just as insular and ignorant as the Morecambrians he so despised — more so, even, as these people had all the advantages of wealth and education denied to those he had only recently left behind.

Thorn was just returning from the bar when his mobile phone began to beep. Excusing himself, he put down the drinks, removed his phone from an inside jacket pocket and exited the pub, leaving Smith in the uncomfortable company of the middle-aged hoorays inside. Less than three minutes later he came back in, gestured for Smith to drink up and went back out again.

Smith drained his whisky in one gulp. He put on his coat and hurried outside to see Thorn, a lit cigarette in his mouth. His face had drawn into a concerned frown as he studied his mobile phone.

'What is it?'

Thorn looked up. 'I think it's time we returned to Morecambe. That was one of my operatives on the phone. It would appear that our headquarters at the Midland Hotel were ransacked not less than two hours ago. Fortunately, I took most of the important files with us when we came here. They're safe at the house. However, some of the reports and the papers have been taken. What worries me is the fact that someone specifically targeted the hotel. It would appear that whoever is behind this madness is on to us.'

'How do you know it wasn't just kids? Mindless vandalism?'

Thorn passed over his mobile phone. 'I think not.'

It was a state-of-the-art mobile phone complete with internet access, digital camera capability and no doubt a hundred other technological functions that Smith could not even begin to understand or appreciate. It was the downloaded digital image that caught his attention, however, for it showed quite clearly the trashed upstairs hotel room, which had been his. The freshly plastered wall just above the head of his bed had been defaced, blood-red letters proclaiming the now-familiar slogan.

★ ★ ★

The thing that had once been Barry Crowley stumbled from the shadows of the basement, the length of thick chain manacled to its left ankle dragging on the cold floor. It was drooling, arms extended, eager to get at the array of bones Hoogstratten had laid out on a trolley nearby.

'Back!' Hoogstratten ordered. 'You'll be unchained and fed soon enough.' He looked to where the third of the unholy trio — the bald, blind horror — stood waiting. 'We're running short of paint. It will soon be time to find a worthy victim once again, but in the meantime I think we should assess how those inquisitive meddlers respond to our latest warning. If they're wise, they'll give up and crawl back into whichever hole they slithered from, knowing all too well that what they now face is far more powerful than anything they could ever comprehend. If, however, they decide to do some more prying, then it will be time to eradicate them. Have no doubt, your time will come again. The dissemination to the damned lives on in you. The messages of despair and loss that you convey are reaching the people. The gospel of discord is being spread to the many, and soon all will know of its greatness — for although the words are invisible, the message is pure. It is the underlying essence of the message that pollutes the psyche, breaking down the barriers between the real and the unreal, the desirable and the feared. Madness has already begun to infect the weak-willed. You, The Messenger of the Old Ones, will return.'

⋆ ⋆ ⋆

A little after eight in the evening Smith sat in the car passenger seat, gazing up at the lights of the grey Pennine Tower, Forton Motorway Services' prominent landmark, waiting for Thorn to come out of the nearby Burger King. His mind was elsewhere, oblivious to the headlights and the constant noise of traffic on the busy M6 as it thundered past close to the car park. Things were getting more and more surreal, and not for the first time he began to think that he had truly lost it. On their four-hour journey north from Oxford, Thorn had talked freely about his various theories and about how he reckoned that something altogether monumental was about to occur in Morecambe; although when asked about specifics, he had little to add. Under questioning, he had informed Smith of the Deep Ones: a race of ichthyic humanoids some claimed existed millions of years ago and, it was believed, lived on in some remote parts of the globe. He had spoken of places that the ex-professor had never heard of — R'lyeh, Y'ha-nthlei and Innsmouth. He had mentioned barely pronounceable names that were equally unfamiliar — Cthulhu, Yog-Sothoth, U'hugiaggoth.

The noise of an angry truck driver arguing with somebody over to Smith's left made him glance in that direction, and for a moment reconnected him with the real world — or at least the world he suspected to be real. Strange, inexplicable things were happening to him. Since handling the panoply of Papua New Guinean artefacts amassed by Thorn, which now resided in a box in the boot of his car, the said things had become more pervasive. He was sure he now saw shadows shifting where shadows had no right to be. Everyday things and events now put him on edge, as though his senses had been heightened to their potential danger — a danger of which the majority of normal people were unaware.

Thorn returned, opened the car door and got inside, handing over a wrapped burger and a portion of fries.

Smith ate ravenously. Once finished, he wiped his hands on the napkin. 'So where are we going now?'

Thorn turned the ignition key. 'Well obviously the Midland Hotel's a no-go at the moment, but I've arranged accommodation elsewhere. You'll like it.' He started to pull out of the car park.

Smith yawned. He was feeling sleepy.

'Can't be far now, can it? Seems as though we've been travelling for hours.'

'Not far. We're about eight miles south of Lancaster. From there it's about a twenty-minute ride.'

Smith closed his eyes and tried to nestle back in his seat and get comfortable. His mind began to drift and within five minutes of leaving the motorway services he began to snore, his head resting on his chest.

In the tenebrous, semi-real state between wakefulness and full sleep, his mind was once again assaulted with a barrage of weird images, not least the illuminated coach that overtook them on the left, the many gawping faces of jungle natives pressed up to its windows. Time distorted; and yet it seemed as though no sooner had it flashed past, than he saw himself looking out at a large bridge that spanned a river. Hanging from its supports and the high fence of its walkway path were many bodies.

Still the images continued.

He was now entering a thick fog; and yet, through the murk he could see a large park. A house was set in the park and as he stared, mesmerised, a crowd of figures exited it and proceeded to a large bonfire nearby, their flaming torches held aloft. There were forms writhing in the fire. Something else — something gargantuan and monstrous — crept into his mind; but before he could fully discern what it was —

'Smith?'

'Eh? What?'

'We've arrived.'

Mumbling, Smith rubbed his eyes before straightening his glasses. 'Where?' For the briefest of moments he thought he was still dreaming, the world outside the parked car shrouded by a thick fog. Yawning, he stretched his legs, cringing slightly as a knee joint popped.

Thorn got out.

Smith joined him, wincing at the strong dead fish smell in the air. It was very cold, probably sub-zero.

'You've been asleep for just over three hours,' said Thorn, glancing at his watch. 'It's now twenty to twelve.'

Smith put his coat on and yawned again. 'Oh? I thought you said it would only take about half an hour.'

'I did.' Thorn lit a cigarette. 'The traffic was bad coming through Lancaster and that's when we hit the fog, but even still . . . I think we've experienced some kind of time slip. Which is interesting.'

Smith groaned. 'Here we go again. More madness in Morecambe. I knew we should have stayed well away from this place. Anyway, whatever weirdness is going on will have to wait till morning. I'm exhausted.' He looked around. 'So . . . just where the hell are we going to stay? And before you answer that, you'd better not say we're camping. To hell with that! I'm freezing.'

'Keep your voice down!' Thorn clicked on a torch. 'Come on, the sooner you give me a hand with some of the stuff in the car the sooner we'll be inside.'

Moaning to himself, Smith started to assist Thorn in getting their travel bags and the cardboard box filled with relics out of the boot. Once done, Thorn switched off the engine, locked up and began to walk along a shingle path. They had been going less than a minute when torchlight up ahead brought them to a standstill.

'Mr. Thorn?' a voice called out.

'Oliver?'

A figure came into view, and as it neared Smith realised it was the young man he had encountered at the Midland Hotel.

Thorn discarded his cigarette. 'Is everything in place?'

'Yes, Mr. Thorn. There wasn't much time to make it welcoming, but — '

'No matter,' Thorn interrupted, handing over his travel case. 'Take these, will you, and help Professor Smith with his gear. It's late and we've had a long drive. I think the sooner we turn in the better.'

Smith eyed the approaching lackey with blatant disdain. 'Here, take this.' He handed him his travel bag.

'Whatever you say, Professor Smith.' Oliver turned his back on them both. 'This way, if you please.'

'Has Edward arrived?' asked Thorn.

'Yes,' Oliver answered. 'He got here about two hours ago.'

'Excellent.'

Edward? thought Smith. Who the hell was Edward? Another stooge no doubt. Despite the fact that he had got some sleep, albeit troubled by the strange dreams he was prone to, he was still very tired; and discovering who this Edward character was, was not uppermost in his mind.

The dim shadow of a large mobile home loomed up ahead.

★   ★   ★

Hoogstratten threw the mutant that had once been Barry Crowley his late night scraps before ascending the basement stairs and locking up. He retired to his study, where he would spend a few quiet minutes contemplating, planning for tomorrow and reading a good book. Like *Al Azife* — the *Al Azif* being his current choice.

Later, he would be out in order to daub the walls of some strategic place or other with the message, and he would probably not return from his nocturnal activities until the early hours. In the meantime, it was up to him to see to it that the *Other* was primed and ready for the next kill. Although he himself had access to a tremendous amount of sorcerous ability, it was the *Other* who possessed the vital power; *It* was the only entity capable of fulfilling their joint darkest desires. After all, even the strongest of mortal magicians could not match the strength of an Old One. The subjugation of his will had been painful and the sacrifice of his sanity truly horrendous, but it had been worth it for the gifts granted unto him.

He remembered unearthing *It*. How ironic that had been. His decades-long search for the Holy Grail had continually brought him to this insignificant part of Britain; and his hopes of finding, after so many years, a religious artefact which he could have corrupted to great effect, had at first been dashed. When his spade had prised up the small stone statue, his initial wave of bitter disappointment had been blasted as if by an atomic bomb as the entity within had claimed him.

Nyarlathotep. The Messenger of the Old Ones. The Crawling Chaos. Trapped and bound within the statue.

It was He who had instructed him to gather the nine in the abandoned Winter Gardens. It had been their sacrifice on Halloween that had infused Him with the power to escape from the statue, only to find that a further spell of containment had been woven into the binding. He had been given a pseudo-physicality, but not until all the graves were filled would full spiritual emancipation be attained.

9

Thursday, December 16th, 2004

The living conditions inside the mobile home were far better than Smith had at first feared. It was certainly spacious enough — with three modestly sized bedrooms, a bathroom with a shower, a lounge, a kitchen and a dining area. The bed he had slept in was comfortable and although the room he had been given was basic, it was certainly adequate. Obviously he could find fault if he wanted to, but he opted to just accept things for the time being. After all, what good would come of his complaining? At least it beat sleeping rough in the basement of the Midland Hotel.

After several cursory peeks out of the curtained windows, he had been surprised to discover that the mobile home was in actuality situated at the far corner of a somewhat large and untidy-looking mobile home park. The view from his bedroom window left much to be desired: over to the right and straight in front of him, he could see tall metal railing topped with barbed wire. Beyond this he could see a tangle of trees and hawthorn bushes. It was an eyesore — ripped plastic bags, rubber tyres, torn-out pages from magazines, two rusting shopping trolleys, and other forms of discarded junk lay scattered all around. What looked like a dead baby's head, but was in fact a plastic doll's, lay staring unnervingly from beneath a pile of fire-blackened lager cans. To his left the ground sloped up, a path or roadway of sorts leading towards what he imagined was the main part of the park. At the crest of the hill, in that direction, he could discern the unflattering grey rectangular outlines of several more trailer homes.

The whole place looked dead.

It was raining, rendering the depressing sight even worse.

There came a knock at his door. He opened it.

'Professor Smith. It's just after eight

o'clock. Would you like some breakfast?' Oliver asked. In his hands he held a highly polished metal kettle, and for the briefest of moments Smith was certain he caught a reflection of the grinning cannibal sorcerer's blood-streaked face on its gleaming surface.

Smith stumbled back. 'Eh . . . why, yes.'

'Are you all right, sir?'

'What?' Smith snorted, straightening himself. 'Yes . . . breakfast. Sausages, bacon and eggs and plenty of toast. A cup of tea wouldn't go amiss either. Well, get going.'

'Very well.'

Smith waited as Oliver turned a corner, heading for the small kitchen. He closed his eyes for a moment, willing away the image he had just seen. He walked into the lounge area. Before him, at a rectangular table, sat Thorn and Edward, the man he thought he had been very briefly introduced to last night. He had been tired and his memory was hazy, so he was not entirely sure.

'Morning,' greeted Thorn amicably enough.

'Hmm.' Smith snorted and straightened his glasses. He had no sooner taken a seat when Oliver returned with a cup of steaming tea, which he set down before him. Despite the fact that the curtains in the lounge had been drawn, the light quality outside and inside was poor, necessitating the assistance of two bright standard lamps. From the kitchen came the appetising aroma of frying bacon. In a small bowl nearby lay several plastic jam and marmalade pots.

'We've both had our breakfast, and as we've got a lot to discuss I think it best that we start straight away,' said Thorn. 'Besides, I think we should both hear what Edward has to report. I've heard some of it but I think now is the time to hear the full story.'

Smith added a sugar cube to his tea and gave it a stir before looking up. Despite the fact that he had once been a professional anthropologist, trained and equipped to understand the human condition and thus supposedly an expert in pigeonholing and assessing people, be they civilised, exotic or 'other' — and many in Morecambe were definitely in the 'other' category — he found Edward very hard to place. Age-wise, Smith would say he was probably in his mid-thirties, maybe younger. Being relatively well-built, he guessed that he led more of an outdoor as opposed to indoor life, although there was clearly a touch of the academic about him. Having said that, he wore an Ozzy Osbourne T-shirt which depicted the aging heavy metal star attempting to hitch a ride to Hell; jeans; and a pair of well-walked-in trainers. Beside him rested a small black rucksack.

'Well,' Edward began, his accent unplaceable, sounding like a strange blend of southern Scottish, Lancastrian and American, 'let me just begin by telling Professor Smith a little about myself before I go on to relate what I know and what I've been able to find out about the recent happenings in this area. Although not born in Morecambe, I spent most of my childhood and teenage years here, so I guess you can call me a 'local'. In 1992 I discovered an archaeological site, a mesolithic encampment on

Heysham Head, not far from the cliff-top graves that I believe you both know well. Before I continue, here's something you may find of interest.' He unbuckled a side pocket of his rucksack and removed a small plastic bag. From inside this, he removed a flat CD case and passed it over to Smith. 'Take a look if you please.'

Smith studied the case.

'The Best of Black Sabbath', read the title.

Below this was a photograph of the six rock-cut graves. The whole image was dark and foreboding, the sky sinister and cloudy. In the fifth grave as numbered left to right was a demon or ghost-like entity.

'Coincidence?' asked Edward, noting the look on Smith's curious face. 'The album is a compilation of greatest hits. Although released in 2000, it seems that it *may* in some way portend all that's happening. It's only a possibility though.'

'Edward believes that the strange happenings in the area are not entirely down to the recent murders, but that they are . . . what shall I say . . . focused, or attached to something far older,' commented Thorn.

Edward shrugged his shoulders. 'That's my theory anyway.' He gazed at the ex-professor as he examined the CD case, waiting for him to put it down so that he could have his undivided attention. 'One night I was sat in my tent, busy cataloguing some of the flints which we had unearthed, when this big guy walked in — a South African by his voice. At first I thought he was an interested visitor. Hell, we'd had many turn up to find out how we were getting on and whether we'd found any buried gold and all that kind of stuff. Well, it transpired that this particular character was pretty well clued up on nearly every aspect of archaeology. If he were to be believed, he'd worked on nearly every important site in Africa. He seemed to be very interested in what we were doing and wondered whether we'd found anything of interest apart from flints. He seemed to think that the Holy Grail was buried somewhere nearby — Vicar's Wood, I think he said. I told him that due to the acidic nature of the soil, flints were all that we were finding. Thousands of them. Anyway, he asked who was in charge of the dig. I told him and he left.' He was about to continue when he saw Oliver returning from the kitchen, a tray with Smith's breakfast set upon it.

Without a word of thanks, Smith took his food and began buttering a slice of toast. He nodded to Edward. 'Go on.'

'Well, in short, two nights later I came back from The Royal Hotel to find the campsite deserted. The director of the excavation, Doctor Mark Sallis, had vanished. He's been missing ever since. The police carried out a thorough investigation, but in the end it was just assumed that the pressures of work had got to him and he'd jumped off the cliffs into the sea. I told the police about the mysterious visitor and his strange questions but it fell largely on deaf ears. Anyway, the dig was wrapped up and, coming to the realisation that I might be next for the chop, I hurriedly prepared to leave the area. It was on the last night, I remember — and I was just packing away my tent, all of my colleagues having left — when I saw a strange light up on the ruins. There were figures moving about, hooded figures. There was something very strange about them . . . almost as though they were only half there. I can't describe it any better. I decided to go and have a closer look. Creeping up a path at the edge of the cliff, I could hear chanting as I neared. At the top, I peeked from the cover of the rocks, and that was when one of them suddenly walked straight through me. All I saw was a dark cloak and glowing green eyes. It was like a Nazgûl. You know, from *The Lord of the Rings?* The ghostly feeling was horrible. I still feel it after all these years. I've spent a long time trying to understand what happened, and once I started looking I found evidence for the paranormal all around the world. It was while following up a lead in Germany that I heard about the Hapsburg Foundation and met Mr. Thorn.' He gave a nod of acknowledgement to Thorn before continuing. 'Anyway, to bring matters to the present. I came back to live in Morecambe; and a month and a half ago, on Halloween to be precise, I infiltrated a séance held in the old derelict Winter Gardens.'

'This is where it gets interesting,' added Thorn, noting with some indignation that Smith was paying far more attention to his breakfast than to Edward's tale.

'*Interesting?*' Edward grinned. 'I guess that depends on what piques your interest. Anyway, I snuck in through a side door and found the place eerily quiet. Deathly, yes that's the word I'd use to describe how it was inside. With the light from my torch, I could make out nine figures sat around a small table in the centre. At first I thought that maybe they were drunks or hobos or something, but as I neared I saw that they were all well-dressed. They were all dead, their hands still linked. The look on their faces will no doubt haunt me for the rest of my life. Something had apparently scared them to death. I suppose that's . . . *interesting*.' He glanced at Smith, wondering what kind of reaction his statement would get. When he saw that the ex-professor was preoccupied with munching on a bacon sandwich, he shook his head before continuing. 'Yes. Seems that the poor stiffs had experienced something or other which had killed them right there. Heart attacks was what I initially thought, although from the looks on some of them they had been struck down by some kind of advanced rigor mortis — limbs like stone, petrified almost. Well, needless to say I up and legged it. Got out of there as fast as I could.'

Smith wiped a dollop of tomato ketchup from his chin with a paper napkin and gave Edward a vague look. 'And?'

'*And what?*' Edward turned to Thorn.

'It seems highly probable that what Edward saw in the old Winter Gardens was perhaps the spark or catalyst behind the supernatural activity which infests this area.' Thorn sat back and lit a cigarette. 'Even if one dismisses the fact that nine seemingly well-to-do people died inside that accursed building without drawing any outside attention — no police investigation, no newspaper report, nothing — then one has to surely ask the question, *what were they doing?*' He took a drag from his cigarette.

'Maybe they were raising the ghost of Thora Hird,' interrupted Smith. 'I read in a Morecambe tourist guide that she's supposed to haunt the Winter Gardens.'

Edward gave a derisive laugh. 'I guess that's it. The esteemed professor's hit the nail on the head. Thora Hird's the one behind all of this. I should have known!'

'Come on, let's try and be serious here,' complained Thorn. 'We've got work to do. Important work. And unless we start trying to understand what it is that we're up against, then we might as well vacate this place and head elsewhere.'

'Sounds good to me,' quipped Smith. 'You get the tickets and I'll pack my case. As far as I'm concerned, the sooner we're away from here the better. Since coming here I've been abused, ridiculed, maligned . . . and now, since meeting you, I've become embroiled in probably the weirdest thing imaginable outside a goddamned Stephen King story.' His face flushed, he turned his attention to his sole remaining sausage; and yet, he could no longer doubt that something hideously serious was closing in around them. Between the phantasms of his nightmarish visions and the weird happenings in the so-called real world, a monstrous and unthinkable relationship was crystallising, and only a strong level of vigilance could avert still more disastrous developments.

★   ★   ★

Chrissie West loved jogging, and every morning she tried to get in at least three miles before getting on with the rest of her day. This morning, now that the weather had calmed down somewhat, she planned on doing at least five miles, going from Heysham all the way to Happy Mount Park in Bare and would maybe see about doing most of the return journey as well. All of her route was along the promenade, and thus she had no cars to worry about.

Despite the depressing gloominess and slightly peculiar fishy odour in the air, she had checked her watch and set off in reasonably high spirits. Her spirits were far from high by the time she got back.

For, less than twenty minutes into her

exercise, she noticed something covering a large patch of ground on the promenade. Slowing down, she made her way forward, regarding the messy obstacle with blatant distaste. For a sickening moment she wondered whether there had been some kind of serious accident, the aftermath of which the emergency services had failed to mop up. Fighting back her sense of revulsion, she could see that there were words painted onto the tarmac surface. Words written in what looked like thick tomato-red sauce.

★   ★   ★

'Jumping' Jack Geronimo — real name Kenneth Walker — sat in a half-drunken stupor on a small bench at the Clock Tower, one of Morecambe's landmarks, a plastic bag full of extra-strength lager cans nestling at his worn stirruped boots. He lived in one of the attic rooms of a sordid flophouse along Westminster Road, one of the main roads through Morecambe. His bedroom walls were covered with torn and dated posters of old

Western films; since childhood he had always hankered after the dream of living in the Wild West. He had gone some way to fulfilling that dream when, back in the summer of 1987, the new Morecambe funfair had re-opened under the name of Frontierland; and the original buildings were replaced by ones which, in an inexpensive way, tried to replicate a set from a low-grade cowboy film.

It was here in this artificial environment that Kenneth Walker had 'died' and his alter-ego of J.J. Geronimo had been born. Amidst the ramshackle ticket booths and the remaining saloon, called the Ranch House, an already decidedly strange man from Morecambe had psychologically — and to a great extent physically — metamorphosed into somebody else. Such a transformation, although rooted in an unhealthy fixation with old movies, had started innocently enough when he had secured the highly sought-after position of the furry, supposedly child-friendly, mascot of Frontierland — Frontier Fred. Dressed as Morecambe's answer to Deputy Dawg, Kenneth would lumber around the fairground, shaking hands and hugging boys and girls for many a convenient photo opportunity. He had held this illustrious position for two weeks before developing a bad itch due to the confines of the hirsute face-masked costume, at which point he made a career move to the role of Quick-Draw Mad Dog McGraw — The Fastest, Meanest Gun in the West. Now, dressed as the archetypal 'baddie' — fully outfitted in black — he strutted menacingly from booth to booth and ride to ride, sneering at the kids and chewing imitation tobacco, a set of cap-loaded six-shooters at his hips.

Like most things in Morecambe, however, Kenneth's new character did not stand the test of time; and by the opening of the Easter holiday period in 1988 he was left floundering, unemployed and in desperate need of a job. Pathetically, he had grovelled his way back into employment at Frontierland, working for a while as a lackey on the Arabian Derby stall where, dressed in a white robe, he had presided over the racing of plastic camels. By summer he was set to leave the fairground altogether, disappointed and dissatisfied by the way he perceived its future was being managed when — as luck would have it — a new character, Jack Geronimo, was put forward by the powers that ran the attraction.

Kenneth had the experience and aptly demonstrated his willingness for the role by showing off his acrobatic skills and war cry to the selection panel — even though he was the sole applicant for the position. With a spring in his stride, a chamois, tasselled jacket, a black hat with a red feather, and faked brown skin, he now rushed to and fro, somersaulting and tumbling. His main act involved a staged fall from the rooftop of the Ranch House.

All of that was over sixteen years ago.

Yet, the character had possessed the actor, and Kenneth had now *become* Jumping Jack Geronimo to the extent that he seldom changed his attire and frequently reapplied the bronze fake tan. After the first few years his face had prematurely aged and wrinkled, darkened by the tanning fluid. Heavy drinking hadn't helped his physiognomy either, cracking his skin and turning the whites of his eyes yellow.

Hand shaking, he took a drink from his can of lager.

The Morecambe of his past was gone — consigned to a phase of history no longer willing or able to reappear. Painfully, he had witnessed his hometown's downfall; seen it go through the rocky periods when it looked as though it *might* ascend, only to plummet further into the morass allotted to numerous Northern coastal resorts. Frontierland had crumbled into nothing, its benefactors unwilling to maintain it through its undeniably flagging fortunes, content to let it decay into nothingness.

Mournfully, he cast his sight towards the rusting Polo Tower.

A flash of crimson over to his right caught his vision. There, scrawled onto the wall of the bricked-up public toilets, he saw a swathe of graffiti. A flash of insight in his mind revealed its poignancy to him, encouraging him to get up and go and have a better look.

★　★　★

Mervin Johnson gazed angrily at the thick red lettering that some vandal had painted all over the shuttered door to his cheap premises on the Morecambe front. By trade he was a tobacconist, but in the last few years he had diversified into selling other bits and pieces: walking canes, novelty souvenirs and sundry other bits of equally unwanted tat.

He stood transfixed, his entire body trembling. The writing played on his mind, insidiously crawling into his brain like a malign maggot. The rage within was now succumbing to an altogether different emotion, something more akin to acute apathy and dejection. It was as though a dark and depressing cloud — something drenched in abject nihilism — had descended from the overcast sky, filling him with pessimistic thoughts and hopelessness.

Morecambe was doomed, the message seemed to convey, even though the words *read* nothing of the sort. Rot alongside the resort you lived in, for the time of The King of Worms was fast approaching . . .

The rain lashed at the mobile home, making Smith thankful that they had not ventured outside. It was just after one o'clock in the afternoon and since finishing his breakfast he had retreated to his small room, keen to spend some time alone, away from the three other occupants. He had spent the past four hours reading over some of the collected 'nonsense' that Thorn and his lackeys had accumulated. With the turning of each page it seemed as though he was going over the ramblings of a madman; yet, based heavily on what he had already seen with his own eyes, he knew that some of it was frighteningly true and accurate.

From his understanding so far, it appeared that Thorn believed that who or what was responsible for this unfolding strangeness was operating from perspectives entirely diabolical. Accordingly, what Thorn seemed to be insinuating was that a malign supernatural force was 'engineering' through occult murder and sacrifice an unholy scenario. What exactly the outcome of this ritual was, remained to be guessed at, but it appeared — and was indeed documented via recourse to alleged 'evidence' — that an incipient level of mind-alteration was taking place. Hence, Thorn argued in his theory, the power behind all of this was in some way polluting the sacred area at St. Patrick's chapel with the deposition of murderers — with the intent to befoul the very atmosphere and the inhabitants of the area.

Despite all his readings and his own observations, Smith remained sceptical. Even if one were to accept the notion that occult powers were directly responsible, he found it hard to rationalise both the motive and the *modus operandi*. Why would someone embark on such a crusade? Revenge? Possibly, but against who or what? Was it an act of vigilantism gone wrong — elevated perhaps to a different level, whereby the culprit was indirectly affecting the many with the ritualistic slaying of a few? Was it against an institution, such as the church, or established religion in general? After all, the very act of de-consecration tended to signify the corruption of that which others perceived as being sacred. Could it be that it *was* in some way tied into the proto-pagan worship of the Old Gods, be they Norse or Celtic or something far more archaic? This was a facet he had initially dismissed; but looking back at the images on the hog-back stone, he had his doubts. As to *how* it was being done, well that opened up an entirely different Pandora's Box of impossibilities.

He glanced at some of the notes Edward had jotted down in his neat handwriting. On the face of it, he agreed almost entirely with Thorn, but he did raise some noteworthy points — namely the fact that there seemed to be a direct correlation between the number of sacrificial victims and the increased level of weirdness. Currently, the number of filled stone-cut graves stood at three, from last count at any rate; and Edward believed there had been an observable increase in paranormal activity. Not that he could *see* it, but he had heard strange accounts from numerous sources. There were another five unfilled graves up at the ruins themselves and a possible one near St. Peter's. What would transpire if and when all nine were filled? Would that result in the climax of the ritual — and, if so, what would be the outcome?

Mystery begat mystery, each more terrifying than its predecessor; and the more Smith pondered over his associates' writings, the more he felt that something altogether unnatural and evil was gathering around them. He turned another page and saw a photograph of the red painted slogan he was now all too familiar with:

PREPARE
FOR HE IS COMING

Who, exactly? Satan? The Anti-Christ? Perhaps it was designed merely to perplex and baffle — like something ludicrous from a child's fantasy tale. Everything about this place and the increasing supernatural activity seemed geared to promote insanity — from Eric Morecambe's likeness appearing in an ancient

Egyptian statue, to a demonic West Indian slave-boy wrapped in tape.

How? Why? And who? Those remained the all-important unanswered questions, and Smith doubted whether the answers would be found in the neatly bound dossier of 'evidence' he was currently examining.

There came a knock on his door.

Thorn entered without waiting for an invitation. 'Edward and I are planning to drive up to the ruins as soon as the rain lessens. We'd appreciate it if you'd accompany us. Could be that there's one or two things of interest up there.'

'You mean more bodies?' asked Smith.

'Yes.'

'Thought as much.'

'Well?'

'Well, what? It's not like I have much choice in the matter, is it? You've basically got me exactly where you want me. Isn't that the case, *Mr. Thorn*? I mean, let's face it, you're in deep here, aren't you? All this going on and Christ knows what else; and well, the way I see it, I'm the only one capable of helping out. But, whereas any other man would probably tell you to go and take a jump . . . oh no, not me. Why? Well, because you happen to have me over the old barrel, haven't you? Yes? I say I'm off to the papers with this and, well, I'm branded a raving nut! I can just see it. 'Ex-Oxford professor reappears after three years. Believed killed in Papua New Guinea. Resurfaces in Morecambe and proclaims himself the Witchdoctor General'. Hell! I'd be thrown into the funny farm.'

Thorn just stood there, grinning.

Smith stammered, uncertain how to continue. 'Yes . . . so . . . just remember. This isn't over. Not by a long shot. Reciprocity. Once I've done whatever you want me to do here, you get me on the next plane out. You got that?'

Thorn replied by taking Smith's coat off its hook and throwing it to him.

Fifteen minutes later they were up at the ruins.

'Jesus!' Smith cried. He gazed down at the three full stone-cut graves.

'I take it there are more?' asked Thorn. 'How many?'

Smith looked away. What colour remained in his face poured like water from an upturned cup. He stumbled to one side and dry-retched.

Edward moved to support him.

'How many?' Thorn asked again.

Smith straightened himself. 'These three are full. So with those other two over there that makes five. This first one is as I remember it, but the two to the right of it . . .' He staggered back and retched again, a trail of spittle leaking from his mouth to land at his feet. He dry-heaved. Through glazed eyes, he watched as Thorn paced over to the row of rock-hewn graves and stared in, clearly oblivious to their gruesome contents.

'Any clues as to I.D.?'

'Give him a minute,' said Edward.

Thorn knelt down and began scraping at the nearest grave interior, the one that Smith could 'see' was still occupied by the fleshy remains of one Trevor '**666** on his forehead' Whitcomb. With the aid of a small trowel, he scraped rock residue into a plastic specimen bag.

A long, stringy stream of bile spewed

from Smith's mouth, leaving behind it a bitter, sickly taste. Breathing deeply, he stumbled over to where Thorn worked, scouting for evidence like a demented forensic scientist. He closed his eyes, exhaled and reopened them, hoping perhaps that the gruesome sights would evaporate into the realms of nightmare. Instead, they looked even worse, for he was now taking the time to look over them; and what he saw filled him with revulsion.

The shrivelled cadaver in the grave adjacent to that filled by Trevor was truly horrible, its floppy limbs spread-eagled and overlapping the rims of the vaguely rectangular grave. It was fleshy and boneless, like the others, resembling little more than a pinky-red, baggy protuberance. It was completely devoid of facial or body hair; and despite the fact that it had been sadistically contorted and de-boned, there were no obvious signs of skin breakage — no visible cuts, lacerations or perforations.

There was a foul reek in the air. It was like bad mackerel pâté.

'Well?' goaded Thorn, placing his sample bag into a jacket pocket. 'Tell me what you can see.' He stood over the other grave, staring down unseeingly at its terrible contents.

'It's like the others,' said Smith. 'No bones . . . or at least I think so.' He winced. 'It's just a tangled mess of skin. Male. No other visible anomalies.'

'And the other?'

Smith looked out towards the shoreline. The mist that had lingered all morning was still present, rendering the coast into little more than a shrouded miasma of murky grey tones. From down below, he could hear the sounds of the lapping tide as it crept its dank way towards the cliff face. It was cold, yet clammy — uncomfortable, despite the fact that up here they were exposed to the elements. It seemed as though what sea breeze there was had forsaken them, allowing them to suffer under the fell embrace of the mist.

'Well?' asked Thorn.

Smith just turned and shook his head.

Edward and Thorn spent some time photographing the graves and taking further samples while Smith stared out to sea. At times like this he really missed his habitual bottle of whisky. The prospect of finding more and more 'jellied locals' was forcing him towards a proposition he wished he could avoid. Smith knew there was an alternative course of action and was uncomfortably aware that Thorn probably guessed at it too. The headdress Thorn had lifted from the Pitt Rivers museum pointed towards this. The fact that Thorn had not even hinted at the rite troubled Smith more than if he had boldly demanded it. However, the thought of just continuing to trace bodies and strange happenings — to be forever catching up with some dread vision — did not appeal, and there was a way to find out more if he had the nerve to try it.

A cry broke through Smith's thoughts and he turned back to the graves in time to see Edward fall heavily on the grass.

'What is it?' Thorn demanded eagerly.

'I . . . Jesus, I felt it!' was Edward's stumbling reply. He was rubbing his hand vigorously on the grass. 'Just for a moment I felt the flesh in the grave.'

★ ★ ★

Back in the mobile home, Edward was once again showering following his encounter with the semi-tangible corpse. Smith had been sitting for a while, reading one of the books they had brought from his collection and making frequent notes. Thorn had decided his best contribution at the moment was to pin a large map of Morecambe and Heysham to a board and plot the locations of those unfortunates who had been reported as needing urgent psychiatric help in the last few days.

When Edward had dressed and rejoined them, Smith closed his book and took a deep breath.

'I'll need the headdress, a couple of purified vessels containing earth and water, a spirit anchor and a large vat of blood — preferably human.'

'What?' exclaimed Thorn, looking surprised for once.

'Well maybe not the blood — it's probably more for effect from what I remember, but I do need the rest if this stands a chance of working.'

'What's a spirit anchor?' queried Edward as he rubbed his hair dry with a towel. 'In fact, I feel I've missed a lot here . . . just what are you proposing?'

Smith glanced at Thorn then replied, 'When I was with the tribal shaman in PNG I was allowed to see far more of their rituals than the average anthropologist. They had recognised that I had changed and were curious to see if a Westerner could partake of their mysteries. As I was getting desperate for answers, I agreed. For three months I lived as a neophyte shaman while their elder sorcerer initiated me. It was gruelling, painful, sometimes seemingly ridiculous, but it worked. I was able to enter a trance and travel in the spirit world. I could, with a lot of effort, see the spirit world and interact, to a limited extent, with what I found there. It's similar to the 'real world' but the true nature of places, things and people is far clearer. The elder shamans use this to divine truth, maintain balance, choose good leaders . . . that kind of thing. Or, they can use it to terrorise their enemies.

I've seen men, women and children ripped into pieces and devoured by the vengeful shamans in their spirit forms. It's not nice, not an easy thing to watch.'

'Or to do?' Thorn interjected quietly.

Smith had almost forgotten him; his natural instinct to lecture the young had centred his attention on Edward. Turning now to Thorn, he said: 'I . . . I had an idea *you* might know . . . but I would like to know how.'

Thorn sat on the narrow sofa. 'A few years ago, I received a report from a contact in Port Moresby that a 'white witchdoctor', in itself an anomaly, had gone mad in the jungle. When I investigated further I discovered it was you. The local police had circulated a photograph. You can imagine my shock. I'd last seen you in your office, in bloody tweeds no less — and there you were, naked, save for a few feathers and paint, looking completely deranged.' He lit a cigarette. 'I immediately contacted the authorities, only to find that you had been flown back to England by the local missionary group. I suppose they — '

'The Godbotherers! Oh Christ it would be them. You know, I never knew how I ended up back in Britain. I thought I must have done it myself.'

'What was really going on, Smith? I never could work it out for sure; the shamen all clammed up.' Thorn leant forward, eager to hear the answer.

'I was on the final step of the path, the great test for all initiates, the most dangerous one of all.' Smith broke off, trembling. He appealed to Thorn. 'Look, I really need a drink if I'm going to relive all this.'

Thorn considered him for a moment without moving, but Edward quickly pulled his rucksack towards him and lifted out a half-bottle of vodka. Smith gratefully accepted it and took a long swig, wincing at the taste.

'In the final test, one has to open one's mind, or soul, to the spirits and allow them to become fully real. One has a spirit anchor, usually another shaman, who will call one back at the right time, and all the other shamen watch while you are in spirit form. It's the most terrifying experience that I think exists on this earth, but I was determined to go through it — to really know the mysteries.'

Smith took another gulp of vodka. 'After some arduous preparation I went into the trance, the chanting of the shamen around me dulled, and I was through to the other side. It's almost impossible to describe how it feels — at one and the same time I felt muffled, as if wrapped in cotton wool, and painfully exposed. I could see the spirit world and walk within it. It's roughly analogous with the real world but certain things, time in particular, are totally different. I could move at will between the past and the present. I believe the more experienced shamen can see the future as well, but I couldn't. I saw my younger self, industriously taking notes and making my erroneous observations years ago. I saw the first white visitors to the area and witnessed their violent deaths as the tribes reacted with fear to these newcomers. All sorts of animal spirits roamed around, ignoring me.

'Then it started to go wrong. I was

drawn to the time when the rival sorcerer was killed by the tribe. Watching it again in the spirit world was far worse, as I could see the conjured demons tearing at the man's spiritual body as well as the physical mutilations. At the point of death the sorcerer looked straight at me — the spirit form of me. I think he had crossed into the spirit world in his last moments. I suddenly realised he was trying to form a link with me, like a parasite seeking a host.'

Sweat beaded on his brow. Taking a deep breath, he continued. 'The possibility of having his soul latch onto mine was appalling — horrifying — and I reacted instinctively. I had witnessed other shamen attack things while in spirit form, and I felt a kind of swell within my chest. I flung out my hands towards the sorcerer, and a shock like the recoil of a gun flung me backwards. The sorcerer was dead — in both worlds — and I had been one of his killers.' Pale and wide-eyed, Smith gulped down the last of the vodka as his audience of two watched, transfixed, by his story.

'My nerve broke completely and I fled

back to the here and now, desperate to leave that ghastly scene. The link to my spirit anchor was growing weaker by the second and I was terrified I might get stuck there. As I ran into the clearing where I had started and where my physical body was still sitting, I saw the form of my spirit anchor lying slumped on the ground. I . . . I think he was dead, and I think it was my doing.'

Thorn noticed the increasingly deranged, wide-eyed look as the ex-professor related his past experiences.

'I think he must have had a heart attack or something when I attacked the sorcerer, but I don't know for certain. I can't remember anything between rejoining my body and coming to my senses in the lych gate of a church along the Banbury Road in Oxford.'

Neither Thorn nor Edward wanted to break the silence, and the only sound for a while was the rain outside.

Finally, Thorn cleared his throat and awkwardly but genuinely said, 'I truly am sorry for having instigated that experience.'

Smith sighed. 'You could not have known what would happen, I suppose. If you can really help me to fix this mess I'm in, that will serve.'

'I think you might need to get some sleep before we consider any next steps, but first I would like to reassure you of one thing.' Thorn opened his ever-present briefcase and, taking all the papers out, he released a concealed compartment. Within it there were a few typed sheets, which he handed to Smith. 'My team found out what they could from your shamen and, although there was no mention of what you went through, there was one report of a local 'medicine man' as he appears on the records, who suffered a stroke the day the local authorities found you. He survived.' He passed Smith a photograph which showed an elderly man, a native, looking very out of place in a room Smith recognised as the main medical centre at Port Moresby.

Smith drew in his breath sharply and gasped. 'Yes, that's him! My spirit anchor. I didn't kill him!' He stood and walked unsteadily to his bedroom. 'You're right, I need to sleep for a while.' He turned back at the threshold and addressed Thorn and Edward. 'I propose to enter the spirit world once more and track down the entity that is poisoning this area. I will need someone, probably one of you, to be my anchor. You've heard what can happen so I leave it to you to decide who has the stronger constitution.' Without meeting their gazes, he shut the door.

10

Friday, December 17th, 2004

Morecambe Bay had a well-earned reputation as a cruel and dangerous body of water. It was well known that in places the tide could speed in faster than a man could run, as some twenty unfortunate Chinese cockle-pickers had found out to their peril back in February. Shifting underwater channels and quicksands added further hidden dangers, contributing to its capricious menace. However, in spite of its harshness and its unmerciful nature, some, such as Fleetwood fisherman Matt Scott, loved it and relished its challenges.

Gazing from his small boat as he steered it against the strong wind, turning it back inland, he grinned at the circling seagulls overhead, their shapes little more than dark, swooping shadows against the pre-dawn sky. This early morning's catch of haddock, cod, flounder and dogfish had been poor; this, and the hangover brought about by drinking far too much at his brother's fiftieth birthday party the night before, combined to make him think that perhaps it had been a bad decision taking the boat out. This was his living, however: all he had ever known — the wind, the sea and the smell of fish. It was far better than being stuck in some office or working at a garage as his brother did, even if the money was nowhere near as good. Hell, he would be lucky to bring in a week's haul big enough to net what his brother earned in a few days; and what with all this fishing quotas rubbish . . .

A sudden squall fiercely rocked the boat, water splashing in a huge wave against its stern. A further splash sent gallons of water flooding over the starboard side, running into the main compartments and drenching the floor.

Matt cursed; and with a strength born of years working the boats, he expertly steadied the craft once more, riding the waves and bringing the vessel back around, safely directing her towards the coast. At times like this, when the sea was uncomfortably choppy, he often regretted not bringing along a second — as, by maritime law (someone had once informed him), he should. But for him, true deep-sea angling or trawling for shrimps was a one-man job. He had only ever once in the past taken on a second, and that had ended disastrously. The memory of that night when he had gone out with Jim Prattley — an old schoolmate who had fallen on hard times after being made redundant — forever haunted him. Although it had been almost twelve years ago, the memory would never fade, for Jim had been drinking and they had got into a fight on the boat — and Matt had thrown him overboard.

The wind was fairly howling, but he had paid full attention to the coast guard weather report before setting out and he was not aware of anything potentially troublesome. In the distance, through the gloom, he could see the lights of Morecambe and Heysham.

A human-like shadow clambered over the starboard side of the boat.

Yet another mighty wave smashed into the vessel, spraying over the terrible form which, clearly unaffected by the instant deluge, began to right itself. Now standing upright, its bare feet seemingly resting atop the foot or so of water on the main deck, it pointed straight towards the horror-struck fisherman. Long strands of seaweed festooned its glistening naked body. Then its mouth — the sole orifice in its head — opened wide and hell poured forth.

★   ★   ★

'Three more remain,' the terrible, unearthly echoing voice affirmed.

Hoogstratten was startled by the Old One's words. He seldom spoke out loud, preferring, it seemed, to communicate His wishes directly into his brain. '*Three? I thought after this morning's catch there were only two more remaining graves.*'

'*Three!*' He repeated. 'There were nine who bound me, suffocating me in the earth after the traitor deceived me. Nine pious fools whom I destroyed.'

In his mind's eye Hoogstratten saw once again Nyarlathotep's memory of that windswept night.

The nine priests had been waiting inside the tiny chapel where they had carried the statue, performing the ritual of binding which had enabled them to bury Him ten feet deep in the ground close to where the Druid's Stone lay in the nearby wood. His fury at this act had destroyed each of them by the end, incinerating their cassocks, melting their crosses and burning the flesh from their bones, but they had been prepared for it. When the last man fell, the words of the spell taught him by the accursed Elder Gods still on his lips, the link between Him and this world closed — His only escape route sealed by their sacrifice. Each grave was filled with the martyrs' remains and the spectral chain had tightened around Him, leaving Him powerless and tormented by the sanctity of that prison.

'Where is this final grave?' Hoogstratten asked.

'At the new church, close to the grave

marker of the deceiver, the one who lured me to this cursed place — the man from another time.'

From the moment he had disinterred Him from His earthly prison, Hoogstratten had become intoxicated with the Old One's very being and seductive words. To think that there had once been Others like Him, a veritable pantheon of supernatural extra-dimensional beings far superior to humans, who had ruled the spheres beyond comprehension. Neither understood just how and why the Others had vanished. Had the belief in one driven out the many, or had scientific rationalism explained them away? Regardless, He was here with him, His prison having ironically preserved Him down the ages from the irreligious dogma of the modern world. Only a few more days and a few more murders remained until His resurrection would be complete and, uncontested, he would spread His dominion over the planet.

Nyarlathotep went to caress His pet lunatic in the basement and Hoogstratten felt a rush of jealousy, until the screams began.

★   ★   ★

When Smith emerged sleepily at half-past eight, he was surprised to find Thorn talking to a man he vaguely recalled. It was the rector from St. Peter's. He nodded and sat down.

'This is Reverend O'Neil. You remember him? He's got some interesting information.'

O'Neil cleared his throat. 'When I was first appointed in my post, I found an envelope, left by my predecessor. In it was a letter containing helpful information about the area and about some of the parishioners — who likes to do the flowers, the right man to ask about tuning the church organ and so on. However, at the end was a short paragraph that surprised me. It said that if ever I encountered a malign, ungodly force in the church or surrounding areas I was to consult the church records for the year 1835. As you can imagine, I was intrigued and at the first opportunity I dug out the relevant book and started to read.

'There was an account by Rector

Thomas Hannah of a terrible event which he claimed had cursed his family. Apparently, all the rectors down the years had been told that the ground in Vicarage Wood must never be disturbed. I suspect many thought that bodies had been buried there illicitly by a previous rector. It can happen — if a suicide, for instance, had been dearly loved and the family wanted a private burial. Around 1830, the owner of the wood wanted to make a clearing and, despite the warnings of Thomas Hannah, he set some local men to work levelling a mound. By the end of the first day three of the men had fled, claiming that they had felt a ghost trying to 'grab their souls'. Thomas Hannah was duly called in by the now-chastened owner; and as he inspected the ground he felt a very strong 'evil presence' which seemed to be trying to escape somehow.

'Horrified, the man ran back to the church to pray for guidance. He wrote, 'In the third hour of my prayers I began to see things, visions from God. At His prompting I climbed to the ruins of St. Patrick's, where I was overcome by a vision of such intensity that I believed that I was transported in time. I saw a fair-haired man in strange dress handing a crude statue to a priest. The priest was trembling, but on his face there was a look of stern determination. The scene faded. Then I saw nine men gathered in a small stone room chanting in what I at first thought to be Latin. After a while, they filed out of the chapel and stood in a circle in the open air. The most terrible cries and shrieks were to be heard as an unseen spirit railed against their prayers. One by one the men burst into flames, but none faltered. When the last one collapsed I could feel the evil spirit being pulled towards the wood, and the air fell silent.'

He stopped to have a sip of his coffee before continuing with Thomas Hannah's account. ' 'The vision left me and I was back in my church, but the words the nine priests had spoken were engraved on my mind, as were my orders from God. There is of course no monastery here anymore, so I sent for my brothers and cousins for help. I could tell that the spirit

I had felt in the wood was far weaker than it had been in my vision and I hoped that we would not have to share the fiery fate of the nine, but I told every man of the risk. Each went to experience the evil for himself and all agreed that we had a duty, as Christians, to ensure the demon was chained once more.

'We worked quickly but dusk was falling by the time we were ready. I had transcribed the strange verses and taught the others how to speak the words correctly. Each of us carried a crucifix, and after a shared prayer for God's help we set off to the place where the workmen had disturbed the ground. As we began to chant we could feel the presence, and this time I had an impression of a faceless entity. It reached for me but I thank the Lord that it could not touch me. As we neared the completion of the prayers it became angry; I'm sure it tried to send flames down on us, but we felt no more than a slight warmth. With the final word spoken, it disappeared and we sank to our knees with relief. My older brother, William, piled the earth back as it had been before and we returned to the rectory. But our joy at surviving the night and at our success was short-lived. All of us have been inflicted with ill health or bad luck. William was taken from us by a fever and three of us, myself included, have contracted a wasting disease. I cannot but think that these are a direct result of our efforts that night. The evil could not burn us in its weakened state but it has surely cursed us.'

'Hmm. Interesting,' commented Thorn.

O'Neil closed the book. 'I have not known what to think of this account, and at times I have tried to dismiss it as the writings of a poor lunatic — but there are many Hannahs in my graveyard, all dead before or at the age of thirty-two. I now have no doubt that Thomas Hannah was recounting the truth and that the thing that I saw in my church is linked to the malign spirit that he encountered. Additionally, what I felt in Professor Smith that day is a double power, both good and evil.' He turned to Smith. 'You may not be aware of this duality in yourself, but it is definitely there, and I felt it confound the bandaged horror. Whatever evil this statue contained, I believe you could better it.

'I also have the beginnings of a theory about the identity of the malign spirit that Thomas Hannah met and that seems to be exerting its influence once more. After hearing about the ... unauthorised burials at the stone-cut graves, I knew it to be an act of desecration by something that had a reason to hate the church. Although there have been some very strange things happening, there has been no overt, grand unveiling of a supernatural being, which leads me to think that the entity is still partially bound. When the graves have all been defiled, then the last of the chains will break and we will be confronted by its full might.'

Thorn sat up and looked at Smith. 'That being the case, I think the sooner we try the spirit walk the better. I have a candidate in mind for the job of anchor — neither Edward nor myself — and though you may suppose my reasons to be selfish, I truly believe he would be a better choice.'

Jacob Wyzchyck — also known as 'The Watcher' by those few who actually knew him and his obsession — sat, dressed only in his dirty underpants, gazing down from his squalid third-storey bedsit onto Westminster Road below. Hours would pass as he surveyed all with his blank eyes; his binoculars, bag of popcorn and large bottle of vodka resting on the table close by. Over the course of his lifetime in Morecambe he had seen many things — most mundane and insignificant, some far less so. He had witnessed gang fights, break-ins, muggings, drug dealers peddling their wares, car thefts, countless acts of public indecency and two murders. In his capacity as resident voyeur, he had also watched, unseen, as the likes of Jumping Jack Geronimo and a veritable host of other weirdos had gone about their lives.

Last night he had experienced the worst nightmare he had ever had — one that had been so powerful and disturbing in its imagery that he had spent most of the morning wondering if it had driven him truly insane. That in itself confused him. For, in the absence of others, would someone who had been driven insane *know* that they had been driven insane? There had been blood and carnage, that much he remembered all too vividly. There had also been a man without eyes — something horrible that had spoken to him, telling him to join Him.

The sounds of a police siren temporarily broke him away from his strange thoughts.

Down on the street below, two police cars and a riot van sped around a corner, tyres screeching to a sudden halt outside the door to the notorious 'Brown House', one of Morecambe's more prominent and conspicuous criminal establishments. The things that were alleged to have gone on in there would have made the activities of the various Hellfire Clubs seem like an elderly aunt's afternoon tea party.

Five policemen exited the riot van. They were all armed with batons and shatter-proof polycarbonate shields. One shook a can of pepper spray. All wore protective body armour. Three more unarmed policemen got out of their cars, one with a loud hailer.

Harrumphing, Jacob shifted in his chair in order to get a better viewing position. This unfolding spectacle had potential. He reached for his bag of popcorn, his stubbled jowls wobbling.

Suddenly the front door to the 'Brown House' was flung open and a scrawny, chainsaw-wielding maniac wearing a grotesque clown mask came rushing out. Apart from the mask, he was stark naked. Screaming profanities, chainsaw held aloft, he charged the surprised policemen, cutting one down in a bloody spray.

Jacob stared, his eyes wide in disbelief.

All hell was now breaking loose on the road below as several more crazies poured forth from the 'Brown House'. Some had painted their faces. Others wore bizarre masks, and all were naked. There were at least a dozen of them — armed with hammers and knives — battling with the police, the one with chainsaw having now been disarmed and battered to the ground. He was still kicking and spitting like a rabid dog.

Suddenly, from an upper floor window, a missile was thrown; and a second or two later one of the police cars went up in flames as the petrol-filled bomb exploded off its roof. This spurred the clown-masked lunatics on and, whooping and crying with mixed rage and glee, they renewed their offensive, wading into the policemen with a blatant disregard for either the law or their own safety.

Another Molotov cocktail came flying, cracking off the pavement and leaving a trail of burning petrol. Screaming, two bystanders on the other side of the road ran for cover.

Training his binoculars on the increasingly violent and bloody fracas, Jacob was shocked to see one of the policemen get stabbed in the face. The unfortunate man seemed to glare straight at him, his face gouged wide, before a form blurred past him. Taking the binoculars away from his eyes — thus affording him a wider, if less detailed, view of what was transpiring — he was stunned to see that five of the policemen were now on the ground, either dead or wounded, whilst all of the

'Brown Housers' were on the rampage.

The nutter with the chainsaw was back on his feet and he stepped over to one of the injured policemen and started carving. Sometime through the screams, the buzzing and the bloodshed, he looked up at the window where Jacob sat and gave him a thumbs-up.

Distant sirens warbled.

★   ★   ★

It was early afternoon by the time Thorn and Smith reached the secure mental unit on the outskirts of Birmingham. As the car drew up outside, Smith was still wondering how to adjust to the addition of a quite possibly insane individual to the situation. He had sat in virtual silence throughout the two-and-a-half-hour journey, desperately trying to think things through — to try and bring reason to something that seemed utterly unreasonable.

'So who is this?' Smith inquired, getting out of the car. 'You've said hardly a thing about this person.'

'The man I've chosen was born into a famous family but left home at the age of nineteen and travelled the globe, apparently seeking out the weird and the wonderful.' Thorn closed his car door, a black folder under his arm. 'Have you ever heard of Ripley's Believe It Or Not?'

'Vaguely. One of my students included Robert Ripley in an essay about early twentieth century travellers and the often distorted tales they brought back about indigenous peoples,' Smith answered. 'I remember seeing a photograph of some Chinese man with a candle in his head.'

'That's the one. Well, Ripley travelled widely and returned with artefacts, stories, photographs, sometimes actual people, and built an Odditorium that owed much to the freak shows of the nineteenth century. He had a showman's passion for the bizarre. I mention him because the man we've come to see was fascinated with the same kind of thing, and he visited all of the strangest peoples he could gain access to.'

'He's going to love Morecambe,' Smith interjected. 'That's one huge Odditorium and the admission's free. It's getting out that's the problem.'

'Without doubt. Anyway, I believe that it was in the West Indies that he became involved in obeah — '

'I know about obeah.'

'Then you'll know it's a form of sorcery similar in parts to voodoo. I think there must be a link with his experiences in the West Indies and his later descent into madness, although he — '

'*Sambo!*' Smith suddenly interrupted excitedly. 'He was a West Indian slave, was he not? I've been wondering why his body, of all the thousands in that area, was chosen to be re-animated. Perhaps the entity we're tracking recognised the son of a witchdoctor or something similar! His bones could be used for occult purposes.' He gazed towards the fairly modern-looking hospital-like building they were now approaching. A woman in a white coat was pushing an elderly man with a pink Mohican in a wheelchair across the front lawn. So this was where the deranged came to weave baskets and catch butterflies, he thought.

'Hmm . . . that's an interesting theory. Well, back to our . . . patient. When his father died in 1998, our man, who was now in his fifties, abandoned his former lifestyle and took over the family business, successfully at first. However, he soon began to replace key personnel at the factories with those who were personally loyal to him, and the scheme which I had to thwart was set in motion around 2000.'

Smith groaned as realisation dawned. '*Oh Christ!* It's that chocolate-nutter! Jasper, whatever his name is. The guy who's a cross between Willy Wonka and Jim Jones!'

'Yes! Mr. Jasper Darkly. Our friend of old.' Thorn grinned briefly. 'The doctors here are of the opinion that he's pleasant, intelligent, highly creative and incurably mad. They say that he is normal in most matters, but utterly convinced that an evil creature lies beneath Britain and requires blood sacrifices to appease it.'

'But, didn't you tell me that he was correct? Have you just left him here for over three years, rotting in some nuthouse for actually telling the truth?' Smith was getting worked up. 'Is this what you would do to me if I wasn't needed?'

'*Hold on!* If you remember, Darkly was all set to kill thousands of people to appease this entity. We found two entire warehouses filled with boxes of poisoned Easter Eggs, ready to hit the shelves when we raided his factory. Blackwidow-six was his choice of poison, a rather nasty toxin smuggled from old Soviet stockpiles. Anyway, whether or not he was always unhinged I don't know, but when I interviewed him he was clearly a great danger to the public, and the easiest and most humane solution was to have him committed.'

'Humane?'

'Well, consider the alternatives. If prosecuted for attempted murder, he would have to endure a trial, which would find him guilty as he did not even deny the crime. He would have been mentally assessed and sent to Broadmoor. By covering up the crime and getting him in here we've contained the problem and he is better off.' Thorn looked at the serene, pleasant-looking gardens, admittedly with high metal fences and security cameras marking the perimeter. 'I can think of worse places. In fact, I've worked in worse places than this. As to you, you are not, and have never been, *truly* mad. Quite frankly, if you were going to crack you would have done so by now.'

Smith considered this for a moment, wanting to bring Thorn to book for his high-handedness, for interfering in people's lives. But, to be fair, preventing mass murder did rather even things up, at least where his treatment of Darkly was concerned. Deciding that he had nothing to add to the conversation at this point, Smith strode towards the entrance.

After a brief check with the administrator, they were shown to a small lounge, there to await Darkly. Smith suddenly felt sick: this man's bizarre actions had been the catalyst for his own awful revelations. After an uncomfortable ten minutes, the door opened and Darkly walked in.

Smith had prepared himself for some foaming-at-the-mouth straitjacketed lunatic to be dragged forward by two burly orderlies. Instead, the man that calmly entered the room wore old-fashioned circular spectacles and was rather skinny. His slick black hair was parted down the middle, carefully combed back, and he wore a dark suit that was easily the equal of Thorn's expensive tailoring. He looked at the two men awaiting him with mild interest. 'Good afternoon gentlemen. How may I help you?' he asked. His tone was clipped and polite. He reminded Smith of Arthur Askey, genial yet slightly foolish, and Smith had to remind himself that this man had planned mass infanticide — most of his victims would undoubtedly have been children. And yet, he seemed more likely to break into a rendition of 'The Bee Song' or say 'Hello, playmates!' than imitate King Herod.

'Do you remember me, Mr. Darkly? My name is Thorn.'

'I don't think so. Were you a customer? I had a lot of good customers.'

'No.' Slightly nonplussed at Darkly's complete lack of recognition, Thorn wondered just how to introduce both the past and the possible future.

'Would you like to see what I'm working on? It's rather good, even if I do say so myself.' Without waiting for an answer, Darkly delved into his pocket and produced a large egg, which he handed to Thorn. It looked completely normal until Thorn turned it round and saw a window had been cut, allowing the viewer to see inside the egg to where a miniature tableau had been inserted.

Thorn saw in amazement that Darkly had placed inside two houseflies, painstakingly dressed in tiny clothes, posed as if they were drinking tea. The interior had been painted to resemble a domestic setting. The detail was extraordinary and more than a little unsettling.

'I'm rather pleased with that one, I must admit.' Darkly stroked the top of the egg gently before reclaiming it from Thorn. 'Do you collect insects, or are you perhaps interested in egg-crafting? It's a most fascinating hobby, it really is. I've some things in my room that could get you started. So please, do come along, and I'll show you.' He turned to leave.

Totally thrown, Thorn was for once at a

loss for words. As he struggled to open the conversation Smith took charge, impatiently. 'Mr. Darkly, did you try to create a huge sacrifice to appease a supernatural entity?' he asked in a matter-of-fact-way.

Darkly turned. 'Why yes, of course I did.' He talked quite animatedly, waving his hands. 'They don't believe me here, but it's quite true you know. I knew that if I did not act, terrible things would happen.' He scrutinised Smith. 'You look like my sister. You don't, by chance, live in Stafford, do you? She lives in Stafford. Are you another doctor?'

'*What?* No, I'm a professor actually — or at least used to be — but that's not why I'm here.' Smith had decided to take the lead and assess Darkly for himself; after all it would be *he* who would be relying on the man, not Thorn. There was no doubt he was extremely unbalanced. 'I would be very interested to know how you worked out what was required and why you chose to act as you did, but for now I have a rather urgent request for you to consider. I'm trying to prevent a similar disaster from once more overwhelming this country and you may be able to help.'

Darkly looked rather confused. 'Is it to do with eggs?'

'No.' Smith was getting frustrated but continued to speak levelly. 'It's to do with shamanic ritual.'

'Oh well, then I'm your man.' Darkly smiled broadly and stood to attention.

It took Thorn forty-five minutes to complete all the required authorisations to remove Jasper Darkly from the secure unit, during which time Smith helped the unhinged ex-confectioner to pack some of his belongings. Not all, as Darkly had insisted that he wanted to return to the unit after he had helped them.

'I may well be mad, sir, but at least I acknowledge it,' Darkly told Smith. 'I like it here. There are no bad spirits, the staff are polite and I can do no harm. You *do* look very much like my sister. I was extremely relieved when Mr. Thorn changed the sacrifice, if truth be told, and I know I'm better off not making decisions. My father tried to instil a sense of responsibility and a gift for leadership in me. All he really succeeded in doing was to make me feel guilty for abandoning the family firm and inadequate in running it when he died.' He sighed. 'Ah well, that's all in the past now.'

Frowning, Smith lingered over Darkly's collection of decorated eggs and their strange dead inhabitants. One had a fly dressed as a witchdoctor against a painted tropical background. Another contained five woodlice seemingly watching television in a suburban home. Deciding that he could only take so much of this kind of 'art', Smith picked up a photograph album and began flicking through it. His faint interest was quickly replaced by real enthusiasm as he saw many places he recognised, either from books or from his own travels. Darkly had indeed toured the world. There were pictures of him in most of the places much loved by anthropologists and explorers, usually posing with local people, but the album also contained a few beautiful landscapes and many photographs of cargo cult paraphernalia. It was all very familiar to Smith; and when Thorn returned he found the two men talking animatedly about their experiences.

'Did they show you the trick with the gourd and the *tong* stick? I nearly died laughing! They got me to join in their *Soku* dance. I remember back in the late seventies when I attended a Tlingit potlatch ceremony. They burnt an entire killer whale which had been decorated with . . . '

'And their chief had a passion for marmite when I was there, had it with everything! He was also very keen on *Chewits*, I seem to recall. Strawberry in particular.'

'Good Lord!' Smith exclaimed. 'So you've seen the bearded ladies of Southern Chile as well? I can see that this photo was taken at a time when they were performing their annual fertility rite. Anyway, it's a real eye-opener, to say the least. I found myself covered in — '

'I hate to interrupt, but we should really leave now, gentlemen.' Thorn picked up Darkly's suitcase. 'You can bring the photos along to discuss on the journey.' He ushered the two men to his car, still eagerly exchanging memories. They were like two children discussing their favourite toys.

As they were driving through the security gates, Smith let out a startled cry.

Thorn looked in his rear-view mirror and could see that the ex-professor was staring, transfixed, at Darkly's photo album.

'Who are . . . these people, and . . . where was this taken?' Smith felt bile rising to his throat as he continued to stare at the celluloid image. It showed Darkly in a furlined parka coat standing beside a gathering of shrunken, pale yellowy-green-skinned degenerates with slightly conical-shaped heads, pointed ears and evil, slanted eyes. Aside from the skull and scrimshaw necklaces worn by some, all of the natives were naked, despite the fact that the photograph had been taken in a freezing mountainous setting. A weird-looking temple built from cyclopean stonework with odd sinuous designs formed the main backdrop. The sky was strange, the clouds looking unlike any clouds — even considering the possibility of extreme altitude — that Smith had ever seen. For a brief moment, the image seemed to sway and distort before his very eyes.

'Oh, that's when I visited the Plateau of Tsang on my way to Leng. These are Tcho-Tchos.' Darkly pointed to the hideous gnome beside him in the photograph. 'This gentleman's their lama. I saw him devour a man's soul. It wasn't very nice.' He smiled cheerily and turned his gaze out the window. He started humming the tune to 'Over the Rainbow'.

11

Saturday, December 18th, 2004

It was shortly after seven in the morning, and all had breakfasted by the time the rector joined them. The sitting room was getting cramped, but at least everyone had a seat as they talked through the tasks ahead.

'We'll need to get set up here for the spirit walk,' Smith said to Thorn.

Thorn jotted something down on a pad before looking up. 'I think I should be present when you do this, in case anyone comes blundering in, or in case something corporeal attacks you both during the trance.'

'Definitely,' Smith replied.

Edward cleared his throat. 'I have an extra suggestion that I've been thinking over. We know that this entity — spirit, devil, whatever you want to call it — is trying to fill all the graves with bodies;

and when it does, something bad happens, right? So we know that either the entity, or perhaps some minion, is going to have to visit the graves to squash the flesh into them. I suggest that I and perhaps the rector, if he will join me, should stake out the graves tonight and see if we can observe them at it.'

'Very logical, young man, if a little dangerous,' Darkly commented.

'More than a little! It could be bloody suicide!' Smith exclaimed. 'If you're detected I've no doubt that you would be killed on the spot.' He took a deep breath and lowered his voice again. 'The problem is that I think you also have a point.'

'And don't forget, you've only got three days left remaining before the 'big event',' added Darkly.

'*Only three days?* What makes you say that?' Thorn inquired.

'Well, December the twenty-first is the shortest day. For good or ill, that's the day when this will all end. To be honest, I can't wait. Oh, the excitement! It's almost better than Christmas, and of course it comes earlier. There may not be any more

Christmases if things go badly, and what will all the poor children do then? Just imagine. No more Santa and no more kissing under the mistletoe.' Darkly pulled a blatantly false, sorrowful face. 'The very thought brings a tear to my eye.'

'I think you might be right about that,' Smith agreed. 'The winter solstice. From a ritual perspective that would be significant, especially to a creature of darkness.'

★   ★   ★

The atmosphere in the large debriefing room of the Morecambe Police Station was tense as sergeant Mick Humphreys entered. He was accompanied by the chief constable of the Lancaster force, 'Big Bad' Joe McKenzie — a tall, bald-headed man who had a reputation for 'cracking skulls' when skulls need to be cracked.

'Listen up,' said Humphreys, addressing the twenty or so regular officers. 'We all know that there's been some bloody weird things going on in these parts of late. There have been reports of lunatics coming out of the woodwork left, right and centre. At present, our main focus of enquiry centres around an alleged shipment of a particularly nasty form of drug that the scum on the street are calling 'Hell's Message'. Christ knows why, but there you go. Although we've yet to find a trace of it, it's undoubtedly a powerful Class A — it's got to be. Something's turning your run-of-the-mill idiots into psychos. It's possible it may have been ferried here from either Liverpool or the Isle of Man, but we've nothing really to go by. At the moment, it appears to be confined to Morecambe and Heysham. It's our duty to see that it stays that way. Anyone suspected of being under its influence is to be brought in immediately. No warnings. No rights. Zero tolerance. Just get them inside. Use whatever force is necessary.'

'If we haven't found it, how do we recognise it?' someone asked.

'You weren't there at Westminster Road, were you?' Humphreys replied. 'Believe me, you'll recognise anyone affected when you see them.' His face hardened. 'I've spent the morning writing letters of condolence to the widows of Bradley, Tubbs and Cooper as a result of what those drug-using bastards did yesterday, and some of them are still out there, hiding. We're not working alone here, as chief constable McKenzie has allocated almost half of his force to our efforts, so you'll be working alongside our pals from Lancaster. Again, I can't stress strongly enough — '

The main door opened and a troubled-looking policeman rushed in.

'What is it?' Humphreys asked.

'There's another riot, sarge. We've got reports of several casualties.'

★   ★   ★

It was half-past three when Edward, O'Neil, Oliver and Special Agents Clarke and Madden — two of Thorn's 'heavies' — made their way up to the old chapel. Thorn had supplied Edward and O'Neil with surveillance equipment to match that of his men: infra-red field glasses and video cameras, walkie-talkies, five powerful torches and a special box of tricks which he said might pick up something. He did not, however, give them the guns and tasers that his two 'men in black' and Oliver carried.

Oliver looked about him. 'We've identified a few decent places to occupy up here. There's a small path just to the side of the ruined chapel where I suggest we place Clarke and the rector. Edward and I will dig in behind the bushes a little down the slope and Madden will hide beneath the cliff edge. That way none of us can be seen from the graves.'

Edward took up the instructions. 'If you're in immediate danger then make damn sure you let us all know, and the rector will lead the prayers.' Seeing the looks on Clarke's and Madden's faces, he grimaced apologetically. 'I know, I'm not religious either. However, this one could well be worse than what happened at Chanctonbury six years ago.'

'Point taken,' Madden agreed laconically. The memories of that night still haunted him. However, he always drew comfort from the Kalashnikov AK-47 assault rifle he carried. It might not be that good against 'otherworldly' things, but it felt good to have just the same.

'Don't worry about the strangeness of all this; we've seen and done worse in our time.' Clarke checked his watch. 'If that's all, then I think we should get into position. Mr. Thorn said that this happens sometime after dark and it's pretty dim already. Come with me, rector.'

They quickly went to their respective spots and settled down to wait. The cold grew as it got darker and Edward was glad of the fleece under his waterproof jacket. Oliver had provided a flask of hot coffee to share. They had all agreed that it was unlikely that anything would happen early on in the evening. There were still a few people about, walking dogs, but these tailed off around five o'clock. Every hour, on the hour, Oliver used the walkie talkies to check in with the others, and all reported nothing worse than the freezing conditions.

It was starkly beautiful up here, Edward reflected. He had always liked it.

O'Neil, sitting awkwardly on the ground and feeling rather uncomfortable with the whole idea of this stakeout, wondered how many of his predecessors had read the records and known about the serpent lying dormant in this holy place. Had they dismissed it as the ravings of a madman, or had they simply prayed that it was submerged forever? He was having trouble correlating his own view of God and religion with the shocking, undeniably supernatural things he had experienced lately. How did God fit into this equation? Was it something inherently holy in the chanted prayers that had bound the thing, or was there some strange science at work?

Only time would tell.

★   ★   ★

While Edward and the others were spending a very cold and nervous night up at the ruins of St. Patrick's, Smith and Darkly were discussing the practicalities of conducting a spirit walk. Their slightly different experiences of shamanic workings needed to be melded into one plan which both could follow.

'This is a remarkable headdress,' said

Darkly, examining the artefact with the eyes of a craftsman. 'I thought it primitive at first, crudely made, but actually when you look closely it's very finely detailed.'

'I know they take ages to make and that there are accompanying chants and rituals at various stages. It's the genuine article, so it should work.' Smith had removed the small table from the sitting room and was testing the floor for comfort. His body would have to stay in a cross-legged position for a long time and he did not want to get cramp. 'Let's run through the ritual, but without actually starting it. Take off your shirt and put on the headdress. Now, you will also be sitting down and we'll start the chant I taught you. Do you think you have it?'

'Yes.' Darkly nodded.

'Good. As I said, we start the chant together, and it will probably take about half an hour to achieve the separation of body and spirit. This is the tricky part for you, as you must keep yourself halfway between the two states. Too far into the spirit form and we will both be loose in spirit; too much in the body, and the link to me will vanish and I will find it very hard to return.'

'I have an idea about that.' Darkly reached for his photograph album and flicked to a page. 'If you see here, this shaman told me that iron is a fetter to the spirit. He was so adept at entering the spirit world that it sometimes happened when he slept, which could be disastrous, so he used to have a small iron ring that he wore at night.'

'I've never heard of that but it sounds like a good idea,' Smith agreed.

'The only drawback is that he wore it around a rather personal part of his anatomy and I don't wish to sound squeamish, but . . . '

'Good Lord! No. It should be sufficient to hold some iron.'

'Yes, I did always wonder about that particular shaman. I fear he embraced the masochistic elements of the ritual rather too eagerly. And there was that business with the tapir . . . '

Smith was beginning to get used to Darkly's rather strange manner. He came across as the typical English eccentric half the time, but there was certainly some-thing else there as well. Something underneath his veneer which was *very* peculiar. The fact that Darkly was not in the least scared or overtly concerned about what they were attempting was strange in itself. He seemed completely aware of the danger but not at all emotionally connected. Perhaps the mad-ness had driven that out of him. Smith did not know and to a certain extent did not care. As long as he could provide the link back to normality, it was sufficient. *Normality* — that was a changeable thing in this place.

'If I get into trouble out there I will be coming back fast. I'm told it can feel like a fairly hefty thump for the anchor so be prepared. And if you get into difficulties with holding the link, tell me for God's sake.'

'How? Will you be able to hear me?' Darkly wondered.

'I believe so, as long as the link is in place. When I last did this I could always hear the shamen chanting in the back-ground.' Smith considered their preparations.

He had two purified vessels, metal bowls in this case which had been blessed by O'Neil, and the earth and water to put in them. He rather suspected these trappings were unnecessary but was not about to miss out a possibly vital aspect of the ritual just because he didn't believe in it. The only other thing they needed was for Thorn to make damn sure no one disturbed them.

Smith had found that his fear of this undertaking was still strong, but that he was almost eager to start. The experience of leaving his body had been extraordinary in Papua New Guinea and, until it had gone wrong, he had found it fascinating. He had been forced to admit to himself that he did possess some power, and it would be a relief if he could identify this malign entity and dispose of it. The idea tickled him with its absurdity — Mandrake Smith, supernatural vigilante! His thoughts were interrupted by the return of Thorn, who had been getting some provisions.

'Read this.' Thorn tossed a sheet of paper to Smith as he set down the shopping bags. 'There are a few around the town.'

Police Urgent Appeal
If you have any information relating to the disturbance in Westminster Road on Friday afternoon we urge you to come forward or call
MORECAMBE CRIMESTOPPERS.

'I asked around and apparently five people were killed and another seven wounded in a street fight yesterday. The police are working on the assumption that those involved were out of their heads on a new drug.' Thorn looked unusually worried and slightly fumbled the cigarette he was trying to light. 'The word from a contact in the local nick is that the people they arrested were mumbling about 'Hell's Message'.' He took a long, much-needed drag on the cigarette.

Smith and Darkly looked at each other.

'Well, are you ready to go through with this spirit walk?'

'We will be by tomorrow. We both have to fast for twenty-four hours and we've only done four so far,' Smith answered.

'Let's hope that's going to be soon enough.'

'Edward and the rector might have some information for us in the morning, but I don't think there's much more we can do tonight.' Smith realised that for once he was feeling more settled than Thorn. 'I need you to be fully awake tomorrow to guard us, so I suggest you get some sleep.'

Thorn smiled wryly as he, too, recognised the switchover in their usual roles. 'Very well. Wake me if the world ends, but not otherwise.'

⋆   ⋆   ⋆

Later that evening, some three miles from where Edward and his associates were lying in wait for the 'Morecambe Murderer' to put in an appearance — and some five miles from where Smith and Darkly discussed their proposed spirit walk — Hoogstratten pulled his black van into a parking space opposite the old Alhambra building. He waited for a car to pass before getting out and going around to the back of the van.

It was dark and very cold.

Hoogstratten's breath was visible and a light snow was falling. Looking all around and seeing no one, he unlocked the rear door. He clambered inside and furtively pulled the door to.

The interior of the van was untidy, filled with all manner of vehicle spares parts, oil cans, lengths of rope, a small step ladder, buckets, various gardening tools, empty boxes, old newspapers, discarded food wrappers, crumpled beer cans, and several changes of clothing.

He began to get kitted out, donning a wide-brimmed black hat and a large ankle-length trench coat from a hook. Fastening the coat, he wound a long black scarf around his neck and lower face before putting on a pair of dark leather gloves. Once dressed, he reached for the flask-like metal canister in which was the special paint, a plastic pot and a large paintbrush.

He exited the van and locked up, eyes continually scanning the dark street for signs of life. All was quiet. Even the late-night drunks and vagrants that usually gathered at the squalid public lavatories on the other side of the road had slinked off elsewhere, no doubt in search of somewhere warmer to bed down for the night.

His footsteps left a trail in the powdery snow that had fallen as he walked briskly down the street and turned a corner into a shadowy alley. It was very dark here, ideal for what he had in mind. He waited for a couple of minutes before unscrewing the lid on the canister of paint and pouring the blood-red, sticky fluid into the pot.

Once Nyarlathotep had revealed to him the process behind the paint-making, it had always fascinated him. To think that what he had just decanted from the flask had been created from the ground bones of a murderer mixed with the extracted remains of an eighteenth century West Indian slave boy whose blood had been tainted by that of a Deep One was in itself weird; but the way in which it seemed to seep and glisten made him think that it was, in its own way, still alive, almost sentient. There *was* life, or perhaps death, contained within the sanguinary solution, and it was powerful — strong enough to hold his mind and instruct him. He knew that its main purpose was to instil madness, both via the message it would convey and by its very substance.

With some measure of reverence, he began painting. It was almost time.

12

Sunday, December 19th, 2004

It was just after half-past seven in the morning when Edward, Oliver, Madden and Clarke returned through the gloom of a very dark dawn. They had dropped O'Neil at the rectory and were wearily divesting themselves of the spy paraphernalia when Thorn opened his bedroom door.

'Did anything happen? Is everyone all right?' he asked intently.

'No, and yes,' Madden replied. 'We didn't see anything or pick anything up with the detectors. Not only that, it's bloody freezing up there . . . and it snowed.'

'I checked the graves before we left, and the empty ones were still empty, so I guess we will have to do this again tonight.' Edward yawned. 'If you can turf our two witchdoctors out of their beds we can all get our heads down. O'Neil said to call him after lunch to arrange tonight. Anything to report here?'

'Blood and mayhem along Westminster Road but other than that, no, not really,' Thorn replied.

'That's not news. Anyway, see you later, and keep the noise down.' Edward left and Oliver, after grabbing a biscuit from the table, retired to his own room to recover.

Thorn shot a brief interrogatory look at Clarke and Madden.

'Just as they said, although that place is pretty atmospheric,' Clarke answered the unspoken question.

Thorn nodded and went to rouse Smith and Darkly, who soon stumbled into the sitting room, leaving their beds to Clarke and Madden. He made a coffee for himself and poured glasses of water for the two older men, still in their fasting period. He felt briefly compelled to turn on the television and watch GMTV or something else equally banal, to bathe for a while in the mundane like millions of others were no doubt doing. Sometimes he wished for a normal, blinkered life, but that was not an option for him now. Once he had truly accepted that much of what humans believe to be impossible was anything but, there was no return; and in truth he did not miss his former ignorance.

As he waited for the others to properly wake up, he read through the latest reports about weird happenings in the area. They were definitely increasing in intensity and in range. He went to the large map on the wall and plotted the new additions. There were now strange reports from further up and down the coast, yet still geographically centred on Morecambe and Heysham. There was no doubt this contagion was spreading; and, as his maps had shown, as this activity was at the epicentre of the UK, the expanding area of infection had the potential of consuming the country. They really needed to find some solution. He hoped it would be possible to either destroy or neutralise the 'entity'; but if not, then Plan B would need to be in place. His superiors in the Hapsburg Foundation always had a Plan B.

Nothing but static and interference came from the van radio as Jill Shackleton twiddled the knob. She was trying to tune it into The Bay radio station in order to get the nine o'clock local news. She particularly wanted to hear if there had been any more 'developments' since the recent sporadic outbreaks of violence on the streets. Although there had been no casualties this time — unlike the fracas that had occurred in Westminster Road — and although the police had been quick to contain the rioting, that did not mean that things were back to normal. Far from it. There had been so much doom and gloom recently. It seemed that everyone she had talked to had their own bad news story. Why even her good friend, Chrissie West, had recently suffered a terrible mental breakdown and had been rushed off to the Moor Hospital for appraisal. 'Gibbering like an idiot' was how Chrissie's agitated sister had described her over the phone.

Unable to get a decent signal from the

radio, Jill started up the engine and drove the van along the main roadway which led from the Hale Carr Lane cemetery gate into the burial ground interior, tyres crunching through the two inches of snow that had fallen during the night. It was still dark outside and very cold, and she found it hard to believe that the sun had supposedly risen over an hour ago.

At fifty-two, she was still reasonably fit and she loved the outdoor nature of her work, ensuring that the three cemeteries under her 'jurisdiction', as she called it, were well-kept and litter free. She was directly responsible for grounds maintenance and burial locations as well as fencing, tree and bush planting, spoil removal, installation of commemorative benches, and headstone-placing; and in a town such as Morecambe, filled with a burgeoning number of the elderly, she was kept busy. It was also her duty to ensure that any signs of vandalism were reported to the police immediately. Two years ago there had been a case of grave-robbing, but the perpetrator, a local man with severe mental problems, had been tracked down to his home on

Kingsway, not far away, and lynched by a group of outraged relatives of the deceased.

She got out of the van.

The cemetery was empty and deathly quiet, like all cemeteries should be, she thought. However, the silence this morning seemed unusual, for normally she would have been able to hear the sounds of crows. It was also far gloomier than she had ever known it, the headstones and occasional graveyard statue little more than shadowy blurs.

She had always been scared by one particular memorial statue which stood over at the far end of the cemetery, close to the outer wall, with its crawling ivy and top embedded in shards of glass in order to keep unwanted trespassers out. *Or to keep them in*, she thought with a shudder. The statue in question was that of a young boy, whose cherubic countenance somehow looked to her evil and sinister. Whether it was just her over-active imagination or something else it was hard to say, but whenever her inspections of the grounds took her down to that corner of the cemetery she had experienced a cold sensation as though it had been watching her. She was loath to turn her back on the thing; and every time she had done so she was certain that when she turned round it would be closer, or that the look on its face or its stance would have changed.

This morning, however, she wouldn't have to go down there — nor would her tasks take her to where her murdered husband lay buried. Bastard! she thought, looking briefly in that direction. He had behaved like a domineering pig and in the end she had snapped, having taken too many years of abuse and cruelty. She had always maintained that she had never meant to kill him, that she had thought that the single stab with the bread knife would only teach him a lesson and that she had acted in self-defence, a plea that had reduced her criminal sentence some-what. Anyway, that was history and right now there was work aplenty to sort out along the headstone-lined paths that radi-ated out from the main aisle. One of her top priorities was to ensure that one of the new plots that had been recently exca-vated was fully ready for use in the morning.

She was just about to head over when a terrible wail from behind her temporarily froze her in her tracks. It was the voice of the dark proclaiming its power over the light — a dread screech which sent a wave of fear through her, for it touched upon the primal fears buried in the marrow of all living beings.

Terror-filled moments passed.

In some recess of her brain she was certain that the statue she feared so much had come to life and was now directly behind her, ready to grasp her around the neck and strangle her with its cold marble hands. Shaking all over, she slowly managed to turn round.

Stood atop her van was a vision from hell: a hideous, bald, eyeless wraith, its right arm outstretched, a scrawny finger with long, sharp black nails pointing straight at her. Luminous green fog swirled around it.

Stupefied, Jill tried to scream. She could feel the flesh on her face tightening. Rivulets of blood dribbled from the corners of her eyes and nostrils.

The atmosphere around her seemed to

freeze. Her heart had ceased beating but she was still alive — or rather, aware — as the hideous form gripped her. Her clothes melted away. The pain was unimaginable as her bones liquefied in an instant, dribbling like mush *through* her skin, only for her skeleton to later materialise *within* the demonic horror.

What had been Jill Shackleton, fifty-two, Lancaster City Council Cemetery groundskeeper, sagged to the ground — sick, yellowy fluid pooling around her filleted form. With an obscene slurping sound, her head caved in, her tongue lolling from the rubbery mask that her face had become. Her limbs were now no more than flaccid appendages. The grotesque heap of puddled flesh quivered. One arm shuddered and flapped like a dying dolphin's flipper as a final strong nervous impulse surged through the repulsive jelly.

★   ★   ★

Repeatedly chanting 'He is coming . . . ', David Butterworth stepped down hard on the accelerator and steered his waste collection lorry down the Morecambe front, leaving a trail of destruction before slamming it straight into the crowd of drunk teenagers waiting at the bus stop opposite where Frontierland had once been. Three of them managed to leap clear as the twelve-ton lorry ploughed through the plastic shelter and those unfortunates who were too slow in reacting, before crashing into the cement wall beyond.

★   ★   ★

Further acts of wanton madness and savagery broke out in numerous homes throughout Morecambe and Heysham as those who had finally succumbed to Nyarlathotep's message went berserk. For nearly two weeks the mental command, inherent in the message, had plagued the Lancashire coastal towns, initially affecting only the weak-willed or the already borderline insane. However, the Old One's time was drawing near and His power had increased in both poignancy and potency. His revelation had proved more effective than a drug and more damaging than mass indoctrination.

★　★　★

At three o'clock in the afternoon, the curtains of the caravan were closed, although there was very little light left to keep out. Everything was dark and gloomy. Oliver had driven Edward, Madden and Clarke up to the rector's house to finish their preparations there. Smith and Darkly had arranged themselves on the floor opposite each other, with purified metal bowls containing water and earth between them. Darkly looked particularly bizarre with the headdress on and only wearing his trousers, with an iron horseshoe in his pocket. Smith was also bare-chested and had used Thorn's highlighters to mark strange patterns on his skin, the pale colours only just visible. Thorn had stationed his chair so that he could see the two men and the door of the caravan. He had also got Madden to set up security cameras all round the area, with monitors in the caravan, so that he could have advanced warning of any intruders. His gun rested on the table in front of him.

'All right, let's get started with this.' Smith found his mouth was dry but his palms were sweaty.

They began to chant, concentrating on the rhythm of the words and focussing their attention on the here and now.

Smith had explained it to Thorn earlier that day, saying that the first stage of the ritual was to start from an ultra-real perspective. Only then could they move to the median section, where both men would be halfway out of their bodies. Once that was established, Smith would go further and Darkly would stay, balanced between the two states.

The room darkened further as the remaining light bled from the sky. Thorn kept a close watch on his monitors and the two men. To him, it seemed like they must both be in a trance, so completely still seemed their bodies. Their breathing was shallow and their mouths moved as they continued to repeat the words of the chant over and over again. After the first fifteen minutes, Thorn knew the mantra by heart. By the time his watch showed him that an hour had passed, he was struggling to stay awake as the sound droned on and on. He was almost dozing when Darkly spoke abruptly.

'Well really, this is most tiresome.'

'We must be doing something wrong.' Smith opened his eyes and cursed.

'What's happening, isn't it working?' Thorn asked.

Smith uncrossed his legs, wincing a little. 'We got to the halfway point but I could not break away properly. I'm doing something wrong somewhere.' He ran his fingers through his hair. 'Let's get off this damned floor and go through it again.' He and Darkly got to their feet and rather creakily sat down at the table.

'Right. We have the appropriate equipment — the vessels and the headdress. We have the correct chant, I'm sure of it. We must have or we wouldn't have got as far as we did. What am I missing here?' Smith racked his brains for answers. He was secretly worried that it was his own reluctance that was holding him back. 'Back in PNG I was bare-chested and there were other shamen present, but they were there to observe — to make it official — so I don't think they had ritual importance. My anchor and I sat just as we have done here, with the bowls between us.'

'How were you sitting? Cross-legged, kneeling?' Darkly asked.

'Definitely cross-legged.' Smith paused and a look of enlightenment appeared on his face. 'On the ground! That's it! We were to sit on the ground, with nothing between it and us. They didn't say exactly, but it may be of importance to be connected to the earth.'

'So we move outside somewhere.' Thorn got to his feet but Smith waved him down again.

'We can't try it again right now. Once the trance is broken you have to wait roughly one day before going again. I'm sorry, but that's what I was told.' Smith sighed. 'It also means that Mr. Darkly and I cannot eat yet. Besides, we'd die of hypothermia out there.'

Thorn squashed his disappointment down. He was getting worried that time was running out and they had made very little progress towards containing or destroying this malign entity. His superiors needed results. What were the next steps? As things stood he would have to call headquarters.

'How about a tent and some portable heaters?' Darkly asked.

'Too exposed and too bloody cold. We're going to be sitting still for a very long time. Something like an empty barn with four walls and a roof, and an earth floor — that would be better, but I haven't seen anything like that round here.'

'What if I can find you an empty house with a garden that's not overlooked and we can set up a temporary shelter?' Thorn joined the discussion. 'I'm sure I can get it warm enough and it would be safer.' *And easier to defend*, he thought to himself.

'Yes, that would do,' Smith agreed, pulling his jumper back on.

'Right, I'll get on to it.' Thorn took his mobile phone and went to one of the bedrooms. As he dialled the familiar number and waited for the phone to be picked up, he thought that if it was time to get Plan B in place, they would need a bit of notice. 'Thorn here. Can you find me an empty house, no squatters, within about a five miles radius? One with a secluded garden. I also need putting through to 'Big' Sammy . . . '

★   ★   ★

Before it got too dark, Oliver, Edward, O'Neil, Clarke and Madden had walked over to Vicarage Wood. After a bit of exploration they found a place where the ground had been disturbed, but neither Edward nor O'Neil could sense anything from it.

They got into position as before — Edward and Oliver together, Clarke with O'Neil and Madden out of sight below the cliff edge.

As he tried to get comfortable on the ground, O'Neil reflected on his day. He had had only had a few hours of sleep after last night's stake-out, as the mid-morning Sunday service was a ritual he did not want to disrupt. As he had stood at the front of St. Peter's, he had suddenly realised that it was exactly one week ago that Smith and Thorn had raced into the church, closely followed by the poor corrupted body of Sambo. One week in which the fears that had been planted all those years ago when he first read about Thomas Hannah had blossomed into reality. His hands were shaking as he gave the final blessing on himself and his departing parishioners. Returning to the rectory, he had found himself repeating the words of the binding prayers. He found them soothing somehow and they seemed to vibrate pleasantly in his head. After a light lunch he had sat down and begun a letter to his successor. The hidden story of his church must live on even if he did not.

⋆　⋆　⋆

It was dark, very dark.

Oliver checked that everyone was in place and then returned to the shelter of the bushes, slightly down the slope. He had brought a second monitor screen with him tonight so that he, as well as Clarke, could check the cameras.

It was lightly snowing.

* * *

'Have you done much of this kind of thing?' O'Neil asked Clarke curiously.

'A fair amount. I've been in this outfit for over ten years and seen some pretty weird things. I've also spent a good many nights watching and waiting for something that never comes.' Clarke grinned. 'One time, we were hunkered in a toy factory near Swindon, trying to record a spirit, when we saw two lads breaking in. Madden saw them and decided to play back, at full volume, some of the weird sounds we had picked up. They were scared witless, couldn't get out of there fast enough. Spoilt the night for ghost-hunting though.' He looked more sombre. 'We've had some hairy times ourselves too. There are some very warped people, and things, in this world. Madden seems fine, but he still refuses to talk about an operation up in the Shetlands that went a bit pear-shaped by all accounts. To be honest, you tend to know very quickly if someone is up to the job, as the light-weights usually throw in the towel after their first field mission. Not me or Madden; we're ex-SAS.'

'Can they do that — just leave?'

'Of course. We're not going to make someone stay on if they're not up to it. Doesn't help anyone. Oh, there's an official secrets kind of thing we all have to sign; but seeing as we'd be branded nutters if we spilled the beans, secrecy is not really a problem. Not that many people do leave, actually. It sucks you in, knowing stuff that other people don't. Now, I think we'd better stop talking, and start watching.'

★   ★   ★

By eleven o'clock nothing had happened, and Edward found he was drifting off. As he sagged against a sharp stone, it jerked him back to alertness, and he was awake in time for Oliver's hourly check-in. After ascertaining that all was still quiet and nothing was showing on the monitors, Oliver suggested they swap everyone's position to keep them on their toes.

'I'd like to scout out that wood again,'

Clarke announced over the radio.

'And I'm going to go to the slopes over there to get to some higher ground,' Madden put in.

'Why don't I take over from Clarke and join the rector? Edward can move to the edge of the wall. From there he can see down the lane as well as over to the graves,' Oliver suggested.

Four shadows moved over the ground, three covering a short distance only; but one, Clarke, moved steadily up to Vicarage Wood. Five minutes later he radioed in.

'I'm in position. All quiet here at the moment.' He settled down to wait.

★   ★   ★

Hoogstratten had felt the summons so clearly that it was like a fish-hook lodged in his brain. Where He led, he would follow. As he picked up the van keys, he heard the half-wit shaking its chains and howling. The order 'Bring it' sounded in his head and he approached the steps to the basement.

The short journey from Sandylands to Heysham Village only took a few minutes.

Hoogstratten was pulling into the village when Nyarlathotep appeared a little ahead of the van. Hoogstratten parked near the green and went out to greet Him, sinking to his knees.

'There are men up there. Interferers.'

'The same ones as before?' he asked.

'No, they seem to have no power. But I will not be trapped again! It will not happen tonight. It will not happen, ever.' A leprous white hand pointed towards the dark wood. 'There is one in there. Take him, and I will get the others.'

Hoogstratten knew how to kill — it was something he had been trained to do and something he rather liked doing. The witchlight the Old One had conjured was distracting his target nicely, hypnotising him so that he did not detect his approach. He crept up behind Clarke, his assassin's footsteps unheard. His strong left hand clamped around Clarke's mouth, pulling his head to one side as the combat knife held in his right hand slit the Special Agent's throat. Blood spurted forth. Clarke's body thrashed as his legs buckled. Hoogstratten knifed him in the back, his hand drenched in blood, before dropping the dying man. He crouched, and with several deep stabs he finished him off. Taking Clarke's dropped handgun he stalked towards the ruins, blending unnaturally into the shadows.

*   *   *

It was Edward who spotted it first. Scanning the path that led up to the ruins with his night vision glasses, he saw a green blob advancing towards him, its shape barely humanoid. His heart lurched as he continued to watch the lumbering form. He flicked the switch on his radio. 'Edward here. Something's coming. Looks big. Over.'

'I've got it on the monitors. Christ, it looks like Frankenstein's monster!' Oliver replied nervously. 'Stay hidden. Are you hearing this Madden? Over.'

'Loud and clear. Watch where it goes,' Madden confirmed.

Edward's nerves were afire with adrenaline. 'Oliver, get here with your gun! Hurry up!' Through his night vision glasses, he could now see that the green shape appeared lumpy. He jumped as Oliver grasped his shoulder.

'I'm going to take it. As soon as it gets up those steps, shine your torch on it, full beam, and I'll put six bullets in it.' Oliver went into a shooters' stance, readying himself.

Time stood still as the two of them waited.

The hefty *thwap* of bare feet on the stone steps became louder.

Edward flicked the torch on and, with a groan that seemed more human than they had expected, thirty-odd stones of Heysham horror shambled from the shadows into view. It was a nightmarish sight, for the thing that had once been Barry Crowley was fully naked and had suppurating rolls of bilious green flesh hanging, nearly severed, from it. Great mottled blotches covered parts of its skin like a voracious mould. Its face was a Halloween mask of murderous madness. The hair from its head was all but gone — the bald scalp beneath a mass of writhing veins. Its eyes were black and soulless. Slavering green froth, it raised a large axe.

'Shoot it!' Edward cried.

Three shots rang out.

With a loud, drawn-out wail, louder than a foghorn, the whole ruins were bathed in a dark, eldritch glow, further illuminating the terrifying ogre with the axe, making it appear even more monstrous.

'Oh my God!' cried Edward. 'Look!'

Standing atop the ruins of St. Patrick's Chapel, His ethereal form silhouetted by luminous green mist against the night sky, was Nyarlathotep, the Crawling Chaos. He raised His partially skeletal arms, almost in a show of exaltation, and screamed His anger directly at the two men.

Edward and Oliver were sent flying, as though hit full-blast by a hurricane. They both struck the far wall, Oliver headfirst. Edward was luckier and managed to absorb most of the impact with an outstretched arm and his left knee. Pain jolted through him. He staggered back and crumpled to the ground.

The grotesque freak with the axe had been hit by all three bullets Oliver had fired, but the damage caused barely registered. Babbling obscenities, it waded forward and chopped down with its axe, burying the blade deep into Oliver's back as he tried to half-heartedly get up.

Scrambling away from the blood-spattered mutant, Edward looked on in horror as it pulled the axe free, Oliver's twitching body lifted somewhat off the ground. It swung the axe down a second time, a third and a fourth, bloodily hacking the man to death as though he were no more than wood fit for kindling.

'In the name of the Lord!' shouted O'Neil, rushing into the fray, his crucifix in his left hand. He stared up at Nyarlathotep, his entire body shaking with fear, his face white with terror. Feebly, he began to recite the prayer of binding.

Like an unholy bird of prey, Nyarlathotep swooped down and grasped O'Neil, lifting him off the ground. The crucifix fell from his grip as he was carried higher and higher. He was then dropped from a height of a hundred feet or so.

O'Neil screamed as he plummeted into the darkness.

Blood-drenched axe in hand, the thing that had been Barry Crowley shambled towards where Edward lay. There was no trace of humanity left in it, none whatsoever. It was now just a psychopathic butcher; a crazed killing machine.

Madden's killing machine was slightly more effective — and a burst of .30-calibre bullets powered by a hundred and forty grains of powder, fired from close range, rent the night asunder much as they did the ex-Mr. Crowley.

Dark green blood and innards sprayed as the abomination was almost blown in half. Spasmodically, it lurched forward before collapsing against the archway of the small stone chapel, flabby arms extended. Like a sinner hoping for sanctuary, it tried to right itself and enter.

A further burst from Madden's assault rifle blasted into the thing's back, propelling it inside. Bile-like blood splattered in a spray all over the thirteen-hundred-year-old stonework.

'Look out!' Edward shouted at Madden.

Instinctively, Madden leapt to one side, narrowly dodging the two bullets shot by

Hoogstratten. He rolled further and fired the remaining round from his clip at the skulking South African. The wall behind which Hoogstratten took cover was blown apart, rock and stone disintegrating as the bullets fired from the AK-47 blasted into it.

Edward managed to get to his feet, the pain in his left leg excruciating. Unbelievingly, he looked up and could see the spectral terror circling like a vulture high above, its shape trailing ghostly vapour.

More shots ripped the night apart. For a moment the sounds of the gun battle were deafening, truly terrifying.

And then Hoogstratten was coming at full pelt, his gun discarded, his combat knife raised in his right hand.

Edward saw the man with the knife run straight for Madden. Briefly, he wondered why his associate was not shooting, then he realised he, too, was out of ammunition. Both men crashed together. Using a well-practised judo move, Madden sidestepped and tripped his attacker, whereupon he delivered a powerful kick to the dropped man's chest.

Hoogstratten still held the knife, and with a cry he plunged it into Madden's right calf. Madden screamed in agony and, stumbling back, he fell, the knife still in his leg. They were both now grappling on the ground, rolling ever closer to the cliff edge. Kicking and punching, Hoogstratten managed to get on top of the Special Agent. His hands clasped around Madden's throat, his nails digging in and puncturing the flesh. His grip tightened. Desperately, Madden reached out. His hand gripped a loose rock and, bringing it up, he whacked it hard against Hoogstratten's face. Blood streamed from below his right eye.

Hoogstratten shrugged off the injury. Viciously using his greater strength, he hauled Madden to his feet and spun him around, turning him to the cliff edge. Forcibly, he frogmarched him onto the slab of rock and its row of six stone-cut graves. Grabbing his foe by the throat, he was about throw the other over the edge when, with a cry, Edward sank the dropped axe right into the back of his head.

Madden scrambled away.

Through glazed eyes, Hoogstratten turned and looked at Edward. Blood streamed from his split skull, the axe embedded deep. He began mouthing blasphemous words, but his incantation was never completed — for suddenly Edward was charging at him, catching him full-on in a flying tackle which sent both of them over the edge.

13

Monday, December 20th, 2004

Smith was sleeping fitfully, dreams of Papua New Guinea mixing with visions of Oxford and Morecambe in his head. A shaman, fully attired in ritual clothes, stepped out of the Pleasureland Arcade, carrying a mortarboard in one hand and a machete in the other. The sound of the slot machines was loud — one had just paid out and was chinking pound coins into the dish. A moment later, Smith realised that the clanging sound was not in his dream, and he hurriedly got out of bed. Thorn beat him to it and unlocked the mobile home door, and Madden fell through, his knuckles bloodied with his frenzied knocking.

'*They're dead, all dead!*' Madden started to moan. 'I managed to hide . . . but what I saw . . . '

'Get up, man!' Thorn ordered harshly,

then gestured to Smith to help him pull Madden to the sofa. He noticed the blood on his lower leg where he had been stabbed. 'Smith, bandages. There's a first-aid box in the kitchen. Now tell me what happened.' Madden seemed to be trying to co-operate, but his mouth would not work and he was shaking all over. Thorn took hold of his head and forced Madden to look at him as Smith set about bandaging the man's leg.

With a long, ragged intake of breath, Madden began to relate how Oliver, O'Neil, Clarke and Edward had met their ends. His voice faltered and he stumbled over the words.

'Are you sure that they're all dead?' Thorn asked.

'Christ, yes!'

'And what about their bodies? Are they recoverable?'

'I wouldn't think so, although there may be . . . *bits*.' Madden grimaced at the memory. 'Clarke was the worst. When that thing turned up with his body, it was bad, but . . . ' he tailed off and reached inside his jacket. He took out the small monitor screen about the size of a paperback, one that Oliver had set up. 'It's all on here. When I decided to run, I grabbed it. The wireless connection held out for long enough to see what it did when there were only corpses left up there. After what I'd seen . . . it made me run faster.'

Thorn picked up the monitor and pressed the right buttons to play back the recording.

Madden covered his eyes. 'I can't watch it again.'

Thorn, Smith and Darkly watched in silence. The glow from the unearthly entity and the torches that their team had carried still lay on the ground, providing some light for the ghastly scene. It was quick and nasty, the deposited remains of Clarke being almost poured into the second-to-last rock-cut grave. The thing then moved to the next shallow grave and regurgitated something into it. It then turned towards the sea and was gone. The monitor continued to show the rock-cut graves and their unsightly occupants for a few seconds, then cut out.

'That could well be one of the most horrible things I've ever seen.' Darkly broke the silence first. His tone was halfway between disgusted and intrigued.

Smith was struggling with nausea and eventually gave up to go and be sick in the kitchen sink.

Thorn had watched the screen pensively. He had seen colleagues killed in action before, but this was appalling. They would have to move quickly to destroy or contain this monster and if they could not do so, then plan B would *have* to be deployed. It should be possible to make it look like an accident — and better to lose a county than a country. Sometimes sacrifices had to be made for the sake of the greater good. Hell, wasn't that the reasoning behind Darkly's plot back in 2001? Darkly stared straight at him as though he had been reading his mind, a knowing look in his eyes.

'I want everyone ready to go in ten minutes. Gather what you need and then we'll leave together. Madden, do you still have your gun?'

'No.'

'There's a spare under my bed and some extra clips. Bring them. We need to stop this thing, whatever it takes.'

'But that was the last grave,' Darkly reasoned. 'It may be too powerful. Methinks it's won.'

'No.' Smith had returned to the room. 'There's one grave left, the stone coffin by the entrance to the church. I'm sure it's part of the nine. In any case, I'm damn well going to try to get this thing.'

'That's settled then,' said Thorn. 'I have the address of the house my researcher said was most suitable. Let's move out.'

It took a short time for them to pack up their belongings, and it was approaching three in the morning when Thorn drove himself and the others to the abandoned house in Morecambe. He parked up, got out of the car, surveyed the empty street and boosted Madden up and over the high garden wall. The locks were quickly taken care of and they were inside.

'It's pretty basic, and there's no water or electricity, but it's reasonably secure; and that old shed in the garden can be used to make you a shelter.' Thorn unslung the two large sports bags he had brought from the car. 'Madden, come and help me with that while these two check we have all the ritual gear. If we've left anything in the caravan I need to know now.'

Thorn and Madden set to dismantling the shed. As the house was near a street light, they found it reasonably easy to see. With a final heave on the old wood, they lifted the roof and walls clear off the concrete base and shuffled it over to be set on the ground.

'I think that will suffice. It only has to last for a few hours. I'll get the generator set up and try out the heaters.' Thorn looked at Madden. 'Do you want to have a rest?'

'No. When I close my eyes I see Clarke.' There was a haunted look in Madden's eyes. 'You do know what happened, don't you?'

'Do you mean, why it chose Clarke for one of the graves? I think so. When you two were at Chanctonbury that time he killed someone, didn't he?'

'Yes. One of our tasks was an assassination job, made to look like the heat of the moment, resisting arrest kind of thing.'

'So, as it was an intentional killing, it was murder. That's why Clarke was not merely killed. We've unintentionally aided its cause.' Thorn grimaced as he considered this for a moment. 'Still, it could have been worse. At least Oliver had never murdered, nor Edward or the rector.'

Madden sighed and pulled his jacket closer. 'What about that South African bastard and that blotchy fat thing? I wouldn't be surprised if they'd committed murder in the past.'

'That's what's worrying me. Anyhow, if you can't sleep you can help me make this habitable. Smith said they should be able to start shortly after midday and I want to have a trial run first to see if we need to change anything. I'd also like to have any changes to the garden complete before it gets light. Less likely for anyone to notice us that way.'

'Have you contacted headquarters to get a clear-up crew out to the ruins?' Madden asked. 'Believe me, it'll be a squeegee mop-and-bucket job.'

'Actually, no. I don't want to bring in anyone else just now. If Smith succeeds in destroying or banishing that thing, I can get the guys to smooth things over. If he fails, it won't matter anyway.'

'Have you been in touch with 'Big' Sammy?'

Thorn nodded.

'Good,' Madden said fiercely. 'I'd rather see this place nuked than have that monster at large. Is the idea to use the power stations? Sorry, I know you can't tell me, but I'm with you all the way.'

'You know the score. Besides, hopefully we may not need to,' Thorn replied, and both men looked towards the house where Darkly and Smith were unpacking the ritual objects.

★   ★   ★

Smith finished placing the last of their gear on the floor and satisfied himself that it was all present. It would be several hours until dawn, and a few hours after that before he could begin the assault on 'He who was coming'; and he was surprised to find that he was no longer scared. He could feel the anger inside him, which had started when he saw the dreadful deaths of the others. This was no longer about appeasing Thorn and winning a flight to PNG. This was about eradicating a loathsome thing before it was too late. He believed that in the spirit world he could do something about it.

'Do you have anything to read?' Darkly asked nonchalantly. 'I seem to recall that you had a very comprehensive library of highly entertaining novels when last I visited you in Stafford. You know how much I particularly enjoy Dickens. I remember I had a most enjoyable time perusing your wonderful collection. We've quite a long wait and I find boredom to be a real killer. I wonder how boredom *can* be a killer, but there you have it.'

Smith shook his head. *What the hell was wrong with this guy?* 'No. I'm afraid not. Only Thorn's reports. I suppose there might be something left behind by the previous occupants. Why don't you go and have a look upstairs? You might find an old Mills and Boon or something.'

'I'll go and explore the house then.' Darkly tap-danced out of the room.

Smith was relieved. He was beginning to find Darkly's overall weirdness and lack of emotional involvement unnerving. Even in a situation as grave as the one they now faced, he seemed completely unflustered. Shaking his head in disbelief, he wandered out to the garden, where Thorn showed him the shed on its patch of snowy ground.

'It's reasonably roomy. There'll be space here for the three of us, with Madden around to keep watch,' Thorn said.

'Will he be all right?'

'He's a tough character. Even if he goes to pieces after this, he won't crack during a mission.' Thorn opened the door to check outside. 'Do you think Darkly's up to it?'

'I hope so, but there's something very creepy about him. At times I forget his history, and then he will say or do something and it all comes back. If he . . . *we* survive this, he really must go back to that secure unit. And what's all this nonsense about a sister in Stafford?'

'Purely delusional. According to his personal history file, he doesn't even have a sister.' Thorn tapped his head. 'Just another facet of his madness.'

'Well, the sooner this is done the better, for all sorts of reasons. Not least of which is the fact that I'm bloody starving. Give me a cigarette, will you?' After lighting up and inhaling the warm smoke, Smith walked round the shed. 'It's a bit rickety.'

'At least the garden walls are strong and pretty high. Besides, Madden will be at an upstairs window where he'll pick off attackers with his gun.'

'Very good.' Smith went back into the house, leaving Thorn to wait for the dawn in whatever way he felt fit. It remained to be seen whether that dawn would be the same as the millions that had preceded it.

★   ★   ★

Morecambe and its immediate geographical environs had now become 'The place that time forgot'. Although some might argue it had always held that accolade, it was now isolated completely from the rest of Britain, both in time and space by an impenetrable barrier of unholy fog. Nothing came out and nothing went in.

Indeed, to the rest of Britain, the whole area had now *really* ceased to exist. Consequently, there were no news flashes alerting the British populace to the events now taking place in Heysham and Morecambe — not that many would have been interested anyway. Nor had there been any military mobilisation in order to counter the supernatural threat.

For the disturbances that had been escalating over the past week or so had now erupted into full-blown chaos. The madness that had begun in Westminster Road on Friday now gripped most of Morecambe and Heysham as lunatics and anarchists rampaged largely unchecked through the streets. Many were naked, their faces masked or painted in weird homage to the entity which was now nearing the apogee of its power. Those innocents who retained a modicum of sanity were hunted down and brutally slain by the roving gangs. Like tribal head-hunters, they took the heads of their enemies and mounted them on gates or garden walls. Other unfortunates were strung up from lamp-posts or doused in petrol and burnt alive.

Much of Morecambe was ablaze, with fires burning uncontrollably from Bare to Heysham, from Torrisholme to the outskirts of Lancaster. Vehicles were torched in the streets and plumes of thick black smoke rose into the dark skies.

Nothing could contain the violence. The children of Nyarlathotep were brainless and crazed, their only remaining mission to establish the Old One's position on earth, and they would die in their attempt to do so. Most were formed from the slimy underbelly of Morecambe society — already semi-psychopathic individuals for whom reality held no attraction or salvation from the drudgery and the leaden monotony of human existence. One could argue that most were already dead long before succumbing to the Crawling Chaos' doctrine. In that doctrine, they had finally been given a meaning — a purpose to their lives which had hitherto been missing. And that purpose was to murder and cause as much mayhem as possible.

One of the fiercest battles that dark day took place along the promenade, where a mob of some five hundred crazies armed with all manner of weapons, ranging from air rifles to kitchen tableware, confronted a roadblock established by those still-sane Morecambrians. The bedlamites, led by Joe McKenzie and a dozen corrupted anti-riot-trained policemen, stormed the hastily flung-up barrier, driving a killing wedge into the defenders. Untold numbers were beaten to death or hacked to bits, their corpses littering the front and the promenade. Running battles spilled out into side streets, where maniacs committed further atrocities.

Close to midday a splinter group of the main horde of face-painted berserkers breached the sane Morecambrians' second line of defence and laid siege to Morrisons. Less than half an hour later Noah's Ark was set ablaze, along with the thirty or so rounded-up Morrisons workers and refugees imprisoned within.

Morecambe's main shopping precinct was blown sky-high when, with an ear-splitting *Yee-ha!*, Jumping Jack Geronimo blew himself up by driving a delivery truck filled with BOC gas cylinders through the

Arndale Centre, cracking open the valves and lighting his stolen cheroot.

Tacky amusement arcades and second-hand bookshops were trashed and set ablaze by the mob. The Dome was bombarded by bricks and bottles before some bright spark decided to set that on fire as well by striking it with Molotov cocktails. Doused in oil and flaming, it soon looked like a large Christmas pudding.

★　★　★

The sounds of the blood-drenched Morecambe streets were more pervasive now, the numbers of angry car horns higher than usual, the raised voices more strident. Thorn had decided that they should not venture out, and the police radio he had tuned into backed up his decision. 'It's definitely escalating. I would guess we have until the end of today before more radical measures are taken.'

'Do your lot talk to the Ministry of Defence?' Smith asked.

'Sometimes, obliquely. It gets a bit political.'

'Do you think the madness will stop instantly if we beat it?' Madden wondered.

'In my experience, madness is rather more enduring than that; but I suppose if it is a supernaturally imposed malady it may dissipate quickly,' Darkly said.

'It's one o'clock,' Thorn announced. 'Time to begin.'

Smith, Darkly and Thorn walked out to the shed, where the heaters had been on for the last hour, creating a pleasant fug of warmth which unfortunately made no real difference to the frozen ground, even without the snow. Madden positioned himself at the bedroom window overlooking the garden, the remainder of his and Thorn's armoury spread out on an upturned box.

Darkly had the headdress on and clutched the iron horseshoe, while Smith was bare-chested and had once again marked the required patterns on his skin. They began the chanting, and Smith felt the disturbing sounds of Morecambe's transformation into their enemy's playground fade away. The light-headedness he felt from fasting was intensified this time, and he found it easier to achieve the first stage of the ritual. Darkly was strongly present in reality and Smith felt he could safely detach himself now. He signalled his intent to Darkly, who nodded. They both felt the temperature in the shed rise as the power built up. Watching them, Thorn could also feel the warmth and went to check the heaters before he realised what was happening. Darkly looked much the same to him, but Smith was somehow different.

Thorn returned to his corner to watch and hope.

★ ★ ★

Like a heated balloon, the physical world before Smith stretched and blistered until it finally burst and the unreality of the spirit world broke through. The sensation he felt was as though he had just walked through a wall of thick jelly — a membranous barrier that clung to him with a viscous pull before propelling him through to the realm beyond.

As his vision adjusted, he saw that he was no longer in the recently-shifted back shed of the abandoned home. His surroundings faded, and even as he watched they faded further until they blinked out of existence. Everything was grey and without form; amorphous. For an unknown time he remained static. He became aware that he was not breathing. At first this sensation caused him to panic, but he quickly regained his composure. With no means of navigating, he chose a direction at random and set off. It was like walking through a dense fog — not in the least similar to his experience in Papua New Guinea, where everything had been all too visible. At times he thought he heard the sound of great beasts trumpeting and galumphing close by, but he saw nothing. The ground beneath him felt very spongy, like walking on a bouncy castle.

Sometime later, the fog became a mist, and he arrived in what he thought was some form of central Morecambe — a pan-dimensional Morecambe that existed at various locations within time and space simultaneously. Many of the buildings and streets had warped into bizarre shapes as though reflected through an array of carnival mirrors. He could see very old buildings superimposed on their newer replacements; ghostly outlines of yester-year imprinted on the brick and mortar. From some buildings a bubbling red liquid poured, frothing from windows, chimneys and doorways. An old church-like structure he was now passing on his right had been covered in large spider webs, the resulting white shape resembling a wrapped-up husk, and he shivered to see a huge black feeler protruding from what he assumed was the main entrance. Shocked and more than a bit worried, he moved on, finding that he could now walk properly on the ground.

Through a veritable warren of decrepit back streets and alleys he went, the sounds of faint screams and tortured wails seeming to come from the very cobbles. It appeared that the town itself, from its foundations up, wanted Smith to hear its cries — for him to hear the tales that it alone knew. But he had neither the time nor the inclination to assuage it; and, ignoring the pleas, the warnings and the lamentations, he passed by. He had come here for one reason and one reason alone.

Morecambe front now came into being before him, swimming to the surface of his vision like an image on photographic paper in its bath of silver nitrate.

The Midland Hotel that had once been his sanctuary was now transformed into a *Through the Looking Glass* image of its former self. Gone now was its vandalised and decaying frontage, replaced instead with a startling brightness and an eldritch effulgence. From inside, Smith could hear the dulcet tones of a 1930s crooner singing 'The Lullaby of Broadway'. As he gazed, a ghostly gathering of men and women dressed in clothes of the age drifted inside.

Muted screams of excitement came from the main promenade and, looking in that direction, he saw that the whole of the Morecambe front had suddenly sprung to life as old-fashioned cars and horse-drawn carriages materialised before his eyes. The ghostly resort was buzzing with visitors and locals, ironically alive in a manner he had not witnessed in the real world. His vision widened well beyond normal human scope, permitting him to take in the whole vista of the promenade from Heysham to Bare. He saw that Morecambe had once had two piers and a tower, never quite on Blackpool's level; and indeed it was not fully built, but it was there nonetheless.

His vision shifted again and the spectral Morecambrians began to dissipate, slowly vanishing like unwanted memories from his mind. Morecambe itself shifted, phasing suddenly into a vibrant shade of purple as the last of the spectres disappeared. And then the sound of hurdy-gurdy music started up, and Smith witnessed a further transformation as much of the front condensed before him — shrinking, downsizing — until his vision became focused on the area that had been the Morecambe fairground. For a brief time, all became shrouded in a dismal tangerine fog which seemed to seep up from the ground. Then a wind gusted and blew the fog away to reveal the fairground beyond in all its vivid, garish glory.

Smith suddenly felt like Dorothy in

The Wizard of Oz when the screen burst into colour. Otherworldly people materialised, gawping at him, clearly recognising him as an outsider; yet there was no sense of malice or animosity levelled at him. On the contrary, they seemed genuinely friendly. In this dimension, it seemed Morecambe folk were nice.

And yet something niggled at Smith.

Beyond the camaraderie and the general strangeness, he was beginning to detect something rotten.

A plethora of weird and wonderful characters spilled out of the fairground. Some came skipping and dancing. A trio of stilt-walkers rose above the crowd, their exaggerated black and white minstrel faces and the various instruments they played seeming more suited to a funeral party in New Orleans. As they came closer, Smith realised that what he had taken to be stilts were actually elongated, spindly legs. They walked past Smith and he barely came up to their knees.

There came an unexpected tug and the ethereal lifeline that connected him to Darkly went taut for a moment. He could see the lifeline now, the glowing umbilicus which attached him to the physical world. Like a silvery ribbon it snaked its way from him into the distance. So long as it remained intact he believed he was safe. Reassured, he continued to explore this weird domain.

Smith walked on, drawn inexorably to the eerie sounds of a calliope machine somewhere in the distance.

The scenes were fading again, shimmering almost like a mirage. The underlying sense of wrongness, of corruption, was definitely there — hiding, concealed within the numerous illusions. It was just a matter of tracking it to its source, but Smith's problems were manifold due to the sheer number of distractions that abounded. For even as he tried to focus and exert his full concentration, the surreal fairground underwent a further metamorphosis, the old-fashioned stalls and rides changing into much more modern attractions.

A large, rickety roller-coaster seemed to spring up from the very ground. The smells of candyfloss, fish and chips doused in salt and vinegar, and toffee apples assaulted his nostrils and spoke directly to his empty stomach in words that were almost audible.

He had the sense that something was hiding just out of sight. All he could see or detect was pure Morecambe so far, and it was brighter and more optimistic than he had expected, especially with the current chaos. He had been anticipating a bleak and violent place. Perhaps this was how it was supposed to be, without malign influences interfering. Sometimes, when he had unwittingly overheard locals chatting, they would talk about the 'good old days', and he had always discounted this as being unrealistic nostalgia; but maybe he had been wrong.

Just how long had this entity's influence been seeping through, poisoning the place?

As if in answer to his thoughts, a cold wind whistled down the street and blew away the cheery, comforting scenes. A dark fog settled and he could only just make out the shapes of buildings. He became more aware of the sea: a steel-grey, wind-lashed presence that began to scare him. As he watched, the disturbances in the water drew together and fountained up, reaching high into the air. A figure erupted from the mighty waterspout, a figure he recognised from the footage of the massacre at the ruins. Like a parody of the ascending Christ, it held its arm out wide. Like a stigmatic, blood flowed from its palms.

Then it vanished.

A new form appeared. It was like nothing Smith had ever seen or imagined. At first he thought it was a huge lobster, with spindly legs and serrated pincers; then it changed into a serpentine form, but with spikes projecting from its body.

'When I came to your world it held such intoxicating possibilities of slaughter, blood and chaos,' spoke a honeyed voice that dripped venom. 'I had only to find a form that humans would follow, and there were so many to choose from. So many of you have the desire to kill and merely need the reason. As soon as the sun is at its weakest and the last of the graves is defiled, I will rise again.'

The monster changed again and Smith leaped back as a copy of himself confronted him on the ground.

'I've been known by many names: Nyarlathotep, The Eater of Heads, The Haunter of the Dark. I was here when time began.' The doppelganger reached into the pocket of its coat and pulled out a bottle of whisky. 'Why not take a drink?' It temptingly offered Smith the bottle.

'*Never!*' Smith spat. He could feel an inner power begin to course through his body, as though his nerves were being charged with electricity. He would face this doomsday sober. 'To Hell with you!'

The shapechanger laughed. 'That means nothing to one such as I. I am eternal. I am Legion. I can be anywhere, any time, any dimension, as I choose.'

'But you were bound once, by humans. You were trapped in that statue for centuries.'

The alien Smith disappeared.

Suddenly a massive nine-headed monstrosity rose up from the bay. Its heads were those of the eight that had been sacrificed; its ninth head, hanging limp and impotent, that of Hoogstratten whose remains had not, as yet, been deposited in the final grave. The heads screamed and blasphemed, snarled and spat venom. That of Trevor Whitcomb still retained its three sixes. Its reptilian body was encased in huge armoured scales and its twin pincers snapped the air.

Smith stared in horror at the demonic hydra. Having once studied The New Testament, he had at first thought this horror was the Beast out of the Sea as described in the Book of Revelation; but that one only had seven heads, whereas this had nine.

He looked very small as the monster towered over him.

It reached for him and dragged him away.

★   ★   ★

Like an angler who had just hooked the world's largest fish, Darkly felt the sudden tug on the spirit lifeline. It was quick, and he had no time to control himself as he was dragged into the unreality of beyond, only dimly aware that Thorn had managed to anchor him. Snaking out into the distance, he could see the umbilicus that attached him to Smith. It then went taut as his surroundings suddenly exploded in a vortex of whirling colours. One moment he was being dragged across what seemed to be a polar ice cap, the temperature freezing him and covering him in frost. The next he was being drawn, at altitude, across a windswept desert. Then he was over a marshy area with large palm trees. Several mud-brick *mastaba* tombs, raised on higher ground, dotted the landscape. A gang of industrious builders looked up quizzically and pointed at him, shouting excitedly in their own language. He waved back.

He speeded up.

Like a fighter jet skimming over the world at a supersonic speed, his surroundings were now no more than flashing blurs. Mountains, oceans and jungles appeared and vanished. Then everything changed and he was dragged through the voids and the dark places, the ethereal link that connected him to Smith stretched to its extreme.

Laughing insanely, he hurtled and spiralled through shadow-filled maelstroms of crackling lightning. He was still laughing as he was tugged through an incarnadine, nightmarish realm of slime-covered, puckered tongues and bulging eyes. Ugly, misshapen jellyfish-like things with long tentacles tried unsuccessfully to grasp him. Something unmentionable, pale and luminous, boiled and bubbled out of a vast stygian abyss . . .

★   ★   ★

The nine-headed nightmare had taken Smith into its lair, where its true presence had festered for aeons. Its functioning heads had taunted him and goaded him. They had spat on him and licked him, covering him in their vile secretions.

Throughout all he had not flinched, well aware that if Nyarlathotep had the power to destroy him, He would surely have done so. His ribs were cracked from its grasp but he could see the Old One remained vulnerable, for His ninth head still hung limp, ineffectually swaying like a pendulum, Hoogstratten's face looking almost pitiful — defeated. Fearful that it would keep him there until it was unstoppable, he knew that if he was to attack it, now was the time. Mustering his own power, Smith began to mumble the words of the *bogay* and the *ogowili* — the ancient Papua New Guinean cannibal witchcraft sorcery he had mastered.

He felt a terrible pain in his right shoulder and, to his horror, realised that something was pushing up through his skin. Screaming in pain, he was revolted at the corruption of his own body. Agonisingly, the head of the cannibal shaman he had helped to kill was forcing its way up. Smith's face distorted as the shaman, whose soul he had unintentionally devoured, shook with rage and tried to break out, to gain control of the body. At this moment in time and space they were joined through a link of mutual spirit consumption — a two-headed sorcerous anthropophage set to do battle against itself.

'*No!* You shall not win!' Smith roared, the horror he had felt three years ago at his initiation channelled this time into anger, not fear. He realised that he had always been subconsciously aware of the parasite and that was why he had wanted to return to Papua New Guinea, to get the tribe to exorcise him. With both hands, he grabbed the protruding head and pulled. The conjoined head screamed. With one final tug, he yanked the head free, the wound in his shoulder gaping obscenely. Resisting the urge to fling it far from him, he started to whisper words of command.

Like a magician shielding the working of his best illusion from view, a dark cloud started to form around him. From out of it there flew the ghastly head, now filled with row upon row of gnashing, shark-like teeth. Two, then three, then half a dozen of hideous, snapping, disembodied heads emerged from the cloud to attack the Old One. Great gaping wounds appeared as they fell upon the enraged interdimensional entity. Where they could, they gnawed and chewed. They tore at Nyarlathotep's scales, eager to get at the softer substance beneath. It was doubtful it was meat, but they targeted it with raptorial hunger all the same. More and more ravenous heads spilled forth, eager to devour.

Viscous ichor poured from the Old One's wounds and it released its hold on Smith. Nyarlathotep screamed, writhing and gnashing. With its pincers, it batted several of the heads away.

Smith shook with tiredness, the magic he controlled sapping his strength.

The Crawling Chaos was in trouble. He knew that now. At full strength He could have torn the feeble being to rags; scattered his spiritual essence to the ends of the universe and the furthest dimensions. But His very strength had always been His weakness. Having no natural foes in any dimension, He seldom had to resort to violence Himself, inculcating others to do it on His behalf. In one last, desperate attempt to survive, He threw Smith as far from Him as possible.

Smith screamed as the spirit line stretched and snapped. Spinning end over end, like an astronaut separated from his capsule, he felt himself being sucked through space.

The cold emptiness of the void beckoned.

★ ★ ★

337

How long he was unconnected he had no means of knowing. It could have been microseconds. It could have been aeons. Nevertheless, it was Darkly who found him, swimming through the midnight-black shadows.

'Take my hand.'

Smith took a hold. 'Who's got you?'

'Thorn.'

Like divers coming up from the deeps before their oxygen tanks ran out, they went as fast as they could, following the spirit line back. One moment they were going vertically, the next horizontally, then spiralling backwards. Everything was shades of grey and dark purple.

Beneath them, like a terror from the deep, screamed the Old One. He seemed to be crawling His way up a dark well, still under attack by Smith's summoned cannibal heads, but they looked faded and were obviously wearing out. Three of the functioning eight heads had been gnawed to disgusting strands. The remaining five reared up to grab them. Just before they reached Smith and Darkly, a deep voice rang out from beside them.

'Stop in the name of the Elder Gods!' it thundered.

Smith saw to his amazement that the ghostly rector he had seen on his first walk into Heysham was facing down the demon. Gone were the placard and the raised crucified figure; instead he was carrying a large metal cross with a cruelly sharpened, spear-like point. Gone also were the rags, his robe now white and flowing. He began to chant and Smith recognised the words.

'It's the binding prayer!' Darkly said in surprise.

'I know,' Smith said. 'And I know who he is. It's Thomas Hannah.'

'Your words mean nothing here!' One of the heads — Jill Shackleton's — squealed with contempt. 'You understand nothing. Your faith can do nothing.' With a huge pincer, Nyarlathotep grabbed Hannah around the waist and started to squeeze.

'And you understand even less!' Hannah shouted. He seemed unaffected, although blood was seeping from him. He raised the sharpened cross and thrust it deep into one of the demon's heads — Bill Dapper's, former funeral-goer extraordinaire.

It screamed and dropped him.

With a cry, Hannah stabbed his crucifix into the monster's thorax. Using both hands, he dragged the holy weapon down, cutting a long gash. The Old One howled as dark entrails poured forth.

Smith and Darkly watched in awe as Hannah repeatedly stabbed into it. The two combatants reminded Smith of pictures he had seen of St. George and the Dragon. St. Michael and the Devil. Heracles and the Lernaean Hydra.

'You *are* allowed to help, gentlemen! I can't beat it alone,' Hannah called out.

Shaking off his shock at the turn of events, Smith pulled Darkly forward. 'Come on, go for the heads.'

'We have no weapons!' Darkly shouted.

'This is a creature of negativity,' Hannah replied, driving his crucifix, spear-like, through a hard scale. 'It abhors goodness and hope. You must — ' Three of the beast's heads suddenly latched on to him, shaking him wildly. The holy lance that the crucifix had become fell from his hands and started to spiral away.

Like an octopus squirting out a cloud

of ink, everything blackened. The dark was impenetrable — bitterly cold, energy-sapping and thoroughly evil. It was the dark of nightmares, in which Smith and Darkly could hear the terrible screams and sounds of rending as the holy revenant was torn apart.

'We must do something!' cried Smith. 'We need that lance. It's our only hope.'

'I'll distract it!' Darkly shouted. 'And let's see if we can't inject a little positivity!' Still holding Smith's hand as they glided towards where the weapon was, he broke into song, his voice pitch-perfect in the cold void: 'Bring me sunshine, in your smile, bring me laughter, all the while. In this world, where we live, there should be more happiness . . .'

A golden glow began to emanate around them. It grew stronger.

The words of the song could not have been more bizarre or more fitting, Smith thought, and somehow they *were* dispelling the darkness. Fighting the desire to start laughing insanely, he grabbed the lance and plunged it into the severely wounded horror.

Nyarlathotep cast Hannah's torn and bloody body aside.

' . . . So much joy, you can give, to each, brand new, bright, tomorrow . . . ' Smith stabbed frenziedly on each downbeat, unholy fluids splattering him.

Darkly was dancing, clicking his fingers to the tune: ' . . . Make me happy, through the years, never bring me, any tears . . . '

The power of the song and the multiple wounds now bore down heavily upon Nyarlathotep. Eight of His heads dangled like dead snakes hung up to dry. One pincer had been half-eaten by the cannibal heads and ichor poured and bubbled from countless injuries.

'*You vicious bastard!*' With a cry of triumph, Smith, covered in demonic gore, plunged the lance into the remaining head, that of some unknown Morecambe murderer. 'I end your existence, once and for all.' He brought the crucifix down one last time, finally silencing the inhuman screams and gurglings.

'Do you think it's over?' Darkly asked.

'I hope so,' Smith panted. 'But we

haven't finished; we have to get back to reality.'

They were almost out, the spirit line winding invitingly before them when it began to fray visibly before their eyes.

'Thorn can't hold both of us,' cried Smith. 'The link's weakening. We're so close, but I don't think we're going to make it.'

'You know something? I think you're right. It's a pity, for we'd make a good double act.' Darkly smiled and somehow detached himself from the umbilicus. Singing 'We'll Meet Again', he spiralled away into the darkness.

★   ★   ★

Smith's eyes opened. His entire body convulsed and a blast of vomit sprayed from his mouth, narrowly missing Thorn.

'You're back, what happened?' Thorn demanded eagerly. He was bare-chested and wearing the headdress.

Smith groaned.

'Smith?' Thorn gripped him by the shoulders. 'Smith!'

343

'I . . . we got it. We got the bastard. I don't think Darkly — ' Smith was interrupted by the loud report of automatic gunfire from upstairs.

'They're on the run!' Madden shouted down. 'They're dropping their weapons. Some are just standing there confused, wondering what they're doing.'

'Cease firing,' Thorn ordered. He took off the headdress Darkly had thrown to him in his last moments in the physical world. He looked tired and drained, even worse than Smith. Darkly himself was slumped on the ground, a mad smile on his face. Smith crawled over to him and checked for a pulse. There was none.

'Shouldn't he be coming round now?' Thorn asked uneasily.

'I'm afraid not. He . . . he turned out to be quite the hero, actually.'

'Is it over?'

'Does evil — true evil — ever die? Thankfully, it wasn't at full strength. Had it been, I don't think we'd have stood a chance.' He briefly explained about the welcome appearance of Thomas Hannah.

'How did he get there?'

'I've no idea, but I'm damn glad that he did. Maybe his spirit had been waiting for a chance to kill the demon who cursed his family. It was his ghost I saw in Heysham. No doubt he had been doomed to bear its message.' Unsteadily, Smith got to his feet. 'I need some fresh air. I'm going outside.'

'It's not safe yet.'

'Since when has life ever been really safe?' Smith retorted, staggering out of the shed. 'Let's see if things are getting back to normal.'

'Wait a minute!' Thorn cautioned, then called for Madden.

They got in Thorn's car and drove to central Morecambe.

It looked like the aftermath of the Apocalypse . . . but it was brightening up a little.

Corpses were everywhere.

Some had been run over, some burnt beyond recognition, others battered to death. A few dangled from lamp posts.

The living looked confused and were wandering rather aimlessly. Certainly, there was no violent behaviour to be seen or heard. Confused men, women and children, suddenly aware of their nakedness, ran back to the safety of their homes.

Madden had brought the little radio with them, tuned in to the police's wavelength. The reports coming in were of riots that had suddenly dispersed. Fights were breaking up and the combatants either collapsing in tears or running away. Ambulances were busy, being dispatched to clean up the wounded, but the threat seemed to have passed. The inexplicable fog that had encased the whole area was gradually lifting.

'I think it's over,' Smith said. 'It feels . . . different. Empty.' He too felt different. He had not realised the weight he had been carrying for the last three-and-a-half years until it was lifted. The shaman had been with him all that time, invading his dreams and poisoning his life; but now he, too, was gone.

14

Tuesday, December 21st, 2004

And so began the clear-up . . .

Epilogue

Monday, May 26th, 2008

The grand re-opening of the Midland Hotel was a day of glamour and hope. The foyer was filled with a big band orchestra. Elderly yet fleet-footed couples whirled to the music. The BBC had thrown a party to kick-start the hotel's new life and everyone, at least for one night, dreamed that Morecambe was on the ascendant once more.

Resplendent in his white tuxedo, Smith, clean-shaven, tanned and healthy-looking, took his iced tea and made his way through the happy crowd. Skirting round Jim Bowen, former *Bullseye* presenter, who was holding court to the camera crew, he walked past the futuristic Rotunda Bar and down the raspberry-pink staircase to the basement. This was where his old squat had been. Pushing through a door, he stepped into a beautiful room with stylised chairs and polished mirrors. He chuckled to himself. It was a set of toilets: swanky, state-of-the-art, expensive soaps included — everything bar the shoeshine boy, in fact — but still toilets.

The strains of Judy Garland's hit 'Get Happy' could be heard even down here. There was no one around so he closed his eyes and concentrated, feeling with his mind.

Perched on one of the chairs was the figure of Jasper Darkly, just as he remembered him.

'Welcome! I'm so glad you made it. I thought we should both be here for this extravaganza.' Darkly greeted him warmly, though his offered hand went right through Smith's.

'When I received the invitation I did wonder if you had anything to do with it.'

'It took me a while to persuade the organiser to send you one. Luckily, I managed to confuse him enough to omit another Mr. Smith and send his invitation to you instead. A small sin I think . . . and isn't it wonderful?' Darkly was spinning gently with his arms outstretched. 'I must show you around.'

'Lead on.' Smith gestured for Darkly to begin, and they started their strange progress. Darkly drifted gently through the doors and the occasional wall, with Smith catching up.

'You must see the restored Eric Gill map of the area; it's superb. Mind the wires. That camera crew have been here all day and the staff keep tripping over them.' Darkly led the way to a long room with a spectacular vista of the sea.

'It is a remarkable transformation,' Smith agreed. 'But I really want to know how you are.'

'Fine. Wonderful, in fact.' Darkly beamed. 'I've so much freedom now, it's truly amazing. After I decided that you, not I, should return, I travelled far and wide through the spirit world.' He chuckled. 'There are some *really* strange things out there! Then I found that I can haunt this world too. Oh, no poltergeist activity or anything tacky like that, but I can watch and it's fascinating.' He paused. 'Did you bury my body?' he asked in a slightly more sombre tone.

'Cremated actually, I think. There were

a lot of bodies in Morecambe that day and I'm afraid we just dragged yours out to the street to join the general clear-up.'

'Very practical. How long did it take before the town was back to normal? I was absent for quite a while.'

'The madness stopped immediately but the fallout took about two months. The Foundation worked hard, quelling rumours and paying others to keep quiet, although most wanted to forget anyway. Morecambe has an amazing ability to forget the unbelievable.' Smith saw that a few people were walking towards him and he strolled out of the French windows to the patio beyond. He did not want them to think he was talking to himself.

The view across the bay was magnificent.

'I work with Thorn now, as it happens. It's an interesting life.' He took a sip from his drink. 'I've just come back from a small coastal town in Ecuador — business, definitely not pleasure.'

'Excellent! I'm so glad.' Darkly was paler in the late sunshine, even to Smith's well-trained eye. Luckily, most people could not see phantoms at all, and a waiter walked right through him.

'Just a moment.' Smith stopped the waiter, a young man with an acne-scarred face. 'You look familiar.'

'I'm just helping out, sir. I normally do the dishes but they wanted more serving staff.' He sounded nervous and the tray of drinks he carried was wobbling slightly. Smith had recognised him but the recognition was one way.

'I've got a good memory for faces. Especially ugly ones.' Smith leaned in close and stared unsettlingly into his eyes. 'A word of advice. Don't ever throw eggs at a tramp again — you never know who they'll turn out to be. 'Pervy' Stan, for example. By the way, that's *Professor* 'Pervy' Stan.'

The waiter's eyes widened. 'I . . . I'm sorry, sir? I . . . ' He stepped back to get out of Smith's range, tripped over the wires that Darkly had gleefully wound around his feet and went careering into a crowd of dignitaries. Glasses shattered and two women shrieked as they were covered in red wine.

The manager rushed over, berating the soon-to-be jobless waiter and signalling for the camera crews to stop filming.

Ignoring Darkly's wicked offer of paying him a surprise visit in the dead of night, Smith just patted the young man condescendingly on the head. 'Don't worry, kid. We're even now.' He walked down the steps and onto the promenade, with Darkly in tow.

The manger's berating of the unfortunate waiter was gradually replaced by the sultry voice of a young female singer drifting out from the hotel, just as the psychic waves of goodwill and hope were transforming Morecambe, for one day at least.

'*There's a beautiful tomorrow, so much sweeter than today . . .*'

We do hope that you have enjoyed reading this large print book.

Did you know that all of our titles are available for purchase?

We publish a wide range of high quality large print books including:
Romances, Mysteries, Classics
General Fiction
Non Fiction and Westerns

Special interest titles available in large print are:
The Little Oxford Dictionary
Music Book, Song Book
Hymn Book, Service Book

Also available from us courtesy of Oxford University Press:
Young Readers' Dictionary
(large print edition)
Young Readers' Thesaurus
(large print edition)

For further information or a free brochure, please contact us at:
Ulverscroft Large Print Books Ltd.,
The Green, Bradgate Road, Anstey,
Leicester, LE7 7FU, England.
Tel: (00 44) **0116 236 4325**
Fax: (00 44) **0116 234 0205**